To Call Ye Forth

Delilah Temple

ASTERIA
BOOKS

2016

To Call Ye Forth (Book 1 of the Witches' Rune Series) by Delilah Temple © 2016

Asteria Books

ISBN: 978-0-9857734-5-8

Cover design by Laurelei Black.

For Katie, Sara, Marcus, and Joe.

To Call Ye Forth

Delilah Temple

Chapter 1

The sacred fume of incense smoke curled and climbed along our altar, filling the temple room with its heady reek. I inhaled deeply, feeling my mind make the subtle shift from this realm into another one. With that single breath, I moved from the world of consensus reality into a place of magic, a place that touches all the realms but belongs to none of them.

My eyes dilated and every cell in my body felt sensitive, open, active. My spirit swayed and danced within and around my body. I was keenly aware of every strand of hair, every inch of skin, every taut muscle. I felt each of my four sisters, my best friends, making her own shift.

Evaline's clear alto voice called out with strong, unearthly notes as she sang the invocation. Haunting. I found her voice haunting, particularly in our ritual circle. "Darksome night and shining moon …." Grace struck a simple beat on her frame drum. A heartbeat to stir the witch blood. "East and South and West and North…." Pearl, shy about her singing voice, added a soft background hum to the vocal invocation. "Hearken to the witches' rune …." Lilly shook a painted rattle, imparting its dry crackle to our magic. "Here we come to call ye forth." My own voice took up the chant of "call ye forth" repeated again and again. It became our anthem, our one thought. The words were layered over each other, harmonized, ever shifting and building.

All five of us were rocking and swaying as we chanted, sang, and played our simple instruments. Seething. This is seething. We pulled energy up into our bodies from the earth below our floorboards, passing the current between us, and sending it spiraling up and around our circle. When it reached a peak, we would send it out into the worlds beyond to accomplish our will in this one. But not yet. For now, we were still building, still seething.

1

I felt the energy snaking up my spine. It lifted me off my ass and onto my feet. My body found the rhythm that was now steadily coursing around the circle. I knew my dance didn't need to be graceful, but years of dance training gave me a great sense of body awareness. I gyrated, stomped, spun, and swayed, pulling each of my "sisters" to their feet to dance with me.

These women, my four closest friends, were my coven. We all knew what magic we worked, and why. We'd taken vows sealed in blood, each at her own initiation, to protect each other and the Craft. A time of need had come, and we agreed to call upon our great teacher and protector to help us overcome the evils tormenting our city.

We call him Robin, this teacher, this magister. He has been called Robin by witches for centuries. Robin Goodfellow. Robin in the Green. Cock Robin. Robin Artisson. Robin Hood. He has been the leader of many covens, sometimes only appearing as a spectral guide, sometimes as a lover in the night to the coven's "maid" or high priestess, sometimes as a rumor on the edge of the wild places. In art, he is shown dancing and feasting and fucking with the wild women who forsake the safety of the town, just for the Sabbat nights, to learn the mysteries of the Craft.

So it was that this night, five witches on the edge of the Circle City gathered to dance naked, to feast, to make love, and to raise the coven's magister. We had each seen him in dreams, in visions. To Grace, he had come as a golden man, radiant like the sun. To Evaline, he had been the green man of the wild wood. To Lilly and Pearl, he had been the "Man in Black," robed in power. To me, the only one of us raised within the sometimes lurid confines of Christian imagery, he appeared red, the classic devil.

I long ago rejected the idea of a red devil hiding under my bed waiting to snatch my soul and cart me off to hell. I believed in Satan, the great Adversary, always working against the Good; but I would have considered myself a fool to call on such a power. Robin isn't that Adversary. He isn't their Satan.

Thoughts of Robin filled my mind. Oh! He had always been so sexy to me. I'd also seen him as my sisters had. Golden, black, green. Always teaching us, showing us new magic, uncovering new mysteries.

We had started the ritual nude. Magic like this, the clothes come off right at the beginning. The chilly little basement room that we use for our rituals was getting warm. More than a little warm, in fact. I lifted my hair as I danced and felt how hot my neck and shoulders had grown. My hair was damp from the dance, but I could feel other areas of my body growing even hotter, even wetter.

I made eye contact with Grace and slid my arms up my torso and to the back of my neck. Grace responded by running her own hands down her soft, curvy frame, lingering over her breasts before skimming her plump little belly and curvy hips. Lilly danced closer to Grace, feeling the pull of the energy as it flared into sexual fire. Lilly touched Grace's rump just as I felt Evaline and Pearl flank me, their hands roaming across my body and each other's.

We were all close enough to touch or kiss any other woman within the circle. We stood for a few moments like this, all hands and hair and breasts and lips. We reached out to each other in lust, in affection, in harmony. Our coven didn't perform sex magic very often, but we produced astonishing results when we did. We were strong women and potent witches, each in our own right. The alchemy of sex raised our natural power exponentially. For the magic at hand, we needed as much energy as we could muster.

The goal is not, as one might assume, to steadily climb toward a frenzy of simultaneous orgasms ending in a collapse of sweaty and spent women. As much fun as that is, it only raises a fraction of the energy we intended to generate tonight. No, what we meant to do was much more intense, much longer-lasting, and much more controlled in its execution.

If we had been dancing in a ring, as witches so often do to raise power, the pattern would be easier to see. One, two, three times around the clockwise circle, then on the fourth time we'd dance counter-clockwise for a third of the circle, then resume our clockwise dance for three more turns before turning back for a bit. On and on, we would dance this pattern. The idea is to raise the energy, raise it some more, then raise it just a little higher before collapsing it back onto itself by just a fraction. Doing this repeatedly produces the most amazing column of energy, but it is best done with a large crowd of people to pack a giant, focused punch.

We weren't dancing in a circle, and there were only the five of us. Our best bet was to use sexual energy, within that same pattern, to reach our goal.

Grace came first. Gracie always comes first. Not a giant, bone-crushing orgasm, but a good thigh-clencher. Lilly had been stroking and fondling Grace with an unrelenting and slow rhythm. Grace's whole body tensed, her Snow White complexion turning bright red with the force of the pleasure. It broke over her in one solid wave of delight, sending her to her knees as she panted and gasped. She would climax again before we were done. Grace had a hair-trigger response. We all knew it. Hell, we counted on it.

While Grace was regaining her breath, Pearl and Evaline turned their attention to each other. Lilly and I kissed and watched and giggled while Pearl and Evie grappled with each other in a lover's wrestling match. The playful struggle for dominance and pleasure was a joy to witness. Evaline pinned Pearl, pushing her thigh firmly between the other woman's legs. Pearl ground and circled herself against Evie's thigh. The giggling stopped as the game turned serious. Pearl moaned, and I knew Evaline's smooth, lithe leg must be slick with Pearl's pleasure. Evie maintained eye contact with her, an intense and furious-looking gaze that dared Pearl close to the edge. Evaline leaned forward, changing the angle of her leg just enough to send Pearl into a mania of ecstasy. Evaline's lips were close to Pearl's throat, and she growled words I couldn't hear before biting the other woman's neck, still growling. Pearl spasmed in orgasm, giggling again as the lusty tension dissipated for a moment.

Evaline rolled away from Pearl just enough to free her leg from the other woman's grip. Evie grabbed her partner's hand and pressed it hard against her own mound as she sprawled onto the floor. I turned my attention more fully to Lilly. Seeing Evaline demand satisfaction in such a forceful way stirred my own passions, and I wanted to start some more intense touching of my own. It wasn't my turn yet. I knew that. If Gracie was always the first to come, I was always the last. I had to have a slow burn to erupt, and I was starting to feel the fire kindled. Lilly and I would stoke the flame together while we listened to the delicious moans coming from our friends.

I love the sounds of fucking. The slow moans, the delicate whimpers, the bellowed roars, and ragged screams. I love the slapping sounds of flesh hitting flesh in steady rhythm. The wet, sucking sounds of intense arousal. I love the breath sounds. Panting, holding, sighing. The sharp inhale as an unexpected pleasure forces its way into the body. Evaline was whining, almost crying, with delight as she and Pearl continue their match. I didn't need to look away from Lilly's kiss to know what the other two were doing. Pearl moaned her satisfaction into Evie's body between the lapping and sucking sounds that I heard just fine.

The room smelled like sex and incense now. Both perfumes were intoxicating. Lilly's long, dark hair tickled my breasts as our mouths met again and again in slow, slick kisses. I glided my hands over her beautiful, bountiful breasts and looked down at them in awe. I am an amply endowed woman, but Lilly's breasts were a marvel. The Neolithic sculptors who carved the clay figurines of ancient mother goddesses with their bulging breasts and round hips must have felt the same way I did right now. She was amazing, and I let my awe of her ripe and full sexiness show in my eyes as I looked back up at her. She threw her head back and gave a throaty laugh before kissing me again. I played with her nipples, and we heard Evaline's orgasm overtake her.

Evie roared and laughed as she came. Twice actually, the second orgasm stealing up on her just as the first subsided. She panted and cried just a little as our dance circled back on itself for a few steps.

5

Lilly and I paused for a moment, letting the column of energy settle into place. I repositioned myself in front of Lilly and draped her legs over mine, which were splayed in a wide V. As I moved into my new place, I saw Grace rubbing her mound so hard and fast that I knew she was quickly approaching her second orgasm of the night. She stared at me with large, lusty eyes before clenching them shut and tensing into another red-faced climax. She breathed heavily and relaxed a moment, but the way she held herself told me she wasn't sated. Our Gracie was going to give us at least one more orgasm before our work was done. She laid herself down between Evaline and Pearl, coaxing each of them into her orbit, as I turned my attention back to Lilly.

I caught her eyes and gave her my sultry-playful look. My nose crinkled a bit and a lusty light danced in my eyes. Hers burned in response. A tiny push against her breastbone told her that I wanted her to lean back against the cushions piled behind her. Dark hair spilled like oil across the pillows and onto the floor. I touched her, endlessly running my hands along every bit of her skin that I could reach. Stretching, I could just reach her nipples, which I pinched and flicked before tracing spirals down her torso and around her hips. I grabbed those hips and squeezed her ass, pulling her closer to me. I pulled myself to my knees and crouched between her spread legs.

I wasn't ready to touch the silken flower of her sex just yet. We were in no rush, and the longer we all touched each other in pleasure, the more energy we would be able to send toward our cause. I continued sliding my hands across her skin, now encircling her inner thighs and pushing her knees up, now using just my fingertips to trace light circles up and down her legs.

I stretched myself up the length of her body, pressing the front of my pelvis against the floor of hers. I could feel the longing radiate out from her. She was ready for a penetrating touch, but she only found the delicious pressure of my body against hers. Instinct made her grind against me, and I circled my own hips in response. I could feel her damp curls against my smooth skin. I leaned over her even further, pressing myself harder against her sensitivity, until I could reach her mouth for a feverish kiss. She titled her hips up to maintain contact while our mouths licked and tasted each other.

The knot of women to our right moaned and writhed in a tangled nest of torsos and limbs. My God, there's a lot of hair to deal with when women make love to each other. Evaline's long chestnut spirals were being held back from her face by Pearl, whose cropped blond pixie cut was probably the best suited to this task. Grace's normally straight black hair was curling in damp waves around her face and shoulders as she thrashed on the floor.

Lilly made a little whining noise, and I knew I was pushing the limit of her patience. With a wicked smile, I pulled away from her, trailing my long auburn curls across her breasts and belly, kissing and licking as I went. I gave her a bite and a wet kiss on her left thigh, then one on her right thigh. She held her breath, her hips still tilted for me. I waited just another moment, relishing the tension in her body and the thrum of energy that it added to our circle. Then, at last, I kissed her. Soft and slow, that first kiss. The tiniest touch of her rosebud with my tongue. I savored the honeyed nectar of her. My kisses grew more intense and more firm as I sought that nectar in every petal of her pretty flower. She was moaning and panting now, and I paid close attention to the movements that pulled throaty moans from her mouth.

Her hips bucked in a spasm of delight, and I slid two fingers into her passage, pressing my tongue flat against her clit. I knew I wouldn't be able to stay here long, but I also knew just how good this felt. I wanted her to have it for as long as I could manage. Her hips and legs twitched involuntarily, and I moaned into her flesh. The vibration of my voice against her sex brought her own moans deep into her chest, her nails clawing at the carpet at her sides. I did it again, shaking my head in a slow "no" and laughing with the pleasure of her delight. Her hips gave a wild lurch, and she raked at my shoulders, pulling me up to her face and kissing me like she was drinking down the last bit of water in the desert. Locked together, we rolled onto our sides, our tongues still frantic to find each other again and again. My hand was still pressed against her, two fingers pumping in steady rhythm. She came in a torrent of heat and slick dew, moaning into my mouth as she did.

Grace followed like one domino toppling the next. Her pleasure must have been deep and satisfying. Her low, raspy moans told me she had finally had her fill of love for the night.

For the last time of the evening, we took those few steps backward in our energetic dance, securing this latest level of the column. We could all feel it as if it were a solid thing in the room with us. I twitched and shook with the electrical tingle of energy, that prickle along my skin and down my spine. My stomach held tension from that current, and I took a clearing breath to make sure my muscles relaxed a little. I didn't want the energy centers in my body to close off because of the tension. I had to be open. I had to be clear.

Evaline pushed a basket of wild-colored make-up pencils into the center of the circle. Everybody grabbed a couple of shades. Everybody but me. I was to be the canvas. I moved the basket and sat down in its place.

"How do you feel, Rose?" Grace asked.

"Ready," I nodded.

I sat cross-legged, shivering despite the heat in the room.

"You're so tense, Rose," Gracie said in concern. "Let's do a quick centering again to relax you." I nodded quickly, my smile more nervous than I had thought it would be.

"Everybody should get centered again," Grace nodded, looking at each of our friends. She closed her eyes, and we followed her example. "Take a deep breath in." She paused and breathed in for a count of four. "And out." Exhaling for four. "In," again. "And out." Pause. "Last time, in." Ah, I felt a tiny release in the muscles of my belly. "And out." We all continued to breathe deeply as Grace moved forward with the short meditation. "Feel your energy like great roots going down and out as you exhale, the energy traveling up and back into the cauldron of your gut as you inhale. Breathe

8

out. Now feel the branches of the same great tree. Up and out, over your head, as you inhale. Back down and into your middle as you exhale. Breathe deep, feeling your energy flow with your breath. Up and down. Out and in."

We sat for a moment just breathing, the room still buzzing with crackles of energy. I stretched and laid myself back, relaxed in the middle of my coven.

"Anything off-limits?" Pearl asked.

"Stay away from my ass," I laughed. "And I'm a little ticklish tonight, so firm touch is best."

For a heartbeat, nobody moved. My eyes were closed, and I stretched a little again. Grace was the first to touch me. She ran her fingers through my hair and traced a pentagram on my forehead with her finger. The others' hands all reached me simultaneously, and I couldn't tell who was who. At first, my mind tried to pick out the texture and pressure of each touch and correlate it to a specific friend. That wasn't helpful. That was me trying to control the experience, so I forcibly unclenched my mind from making sense of it.

I floated on the tide of sensation. Nails, fingertips, hair, and flesh all caressed, flicked, and brushed my skin. Touch like this crosses both hemispheres of the brain and is asynchronous in nature, and it creates altered realities quite fast. The brain kicks over to theta waves within a minute or two, leaving the person experiencing the touch in a euphoric state. It's wonderful for magic.

Someone broke open one of the makeup pencils, and I felt the thick, smooth point leaving its mark on the skin of my pubis. I could feel that it was a pentagram, and my training told me it was the pentagram for invoking earth. Drawn at the root chakra, the energy center that connects into the rich, dark, solid earth. That had to have been Evaline. Next came the water invoking pentagram, drawn by Pearl, just below my navel. My cauldron, the watery womb of life. Next was the star for air, drawn on my throat. Grace. The fire pentagram on my solar plexus, followed by spirit on my forehead, between the eyes. Fire is always Lilly. I guessed that she did spirit, as well.

I could see the colors that I know they must have used. The only colors that make sense. Brown, or maybe black. Blue. Yellow. Red. White.

I tried to let my mind wander again, the hands still roaming as each woman traced her pentagram onto my flesh. Each star had laid a pattern for moving the sexual current through my body, and shooting it like a laser beam through my third eye.

The rest of the symbols that my sisters drew were a mystery to me. I could feel a spiral, maybe. I know there must have been words written in the witches' script, Theban. I trust that each woman marked magic into my flesh, as I felt the others stimulating and caressing me.

Hands pulled gently at my inner thighs, teasing and toying with my yoni. One hand grasped me on that sensitive mound, her fingertips dipping into the growing wetness, her palm cupping my clit. I ground my hips in an instinctive circle. The fingertips spread my own juices across my delicate skin, sending shivers like a ripple through my body.

I felt someone's breath on my chin a moment before her mouth pressed to mine, her tongue probing my lips in a sweet dance as the hand on my sex probed and rubbed those other lips. I moaned into the mouth that was kissing me. She pulled away, giggling. I smiled at Pearl's sweet laughter.

Without warning, another hand firmly gripped the copper curls at the base on my neck, and a growling bite landed just a few inches away. I sucked my breath in sharply as I felt my nipples harden and my sex liquefy into molten lust. The hand squeezed and firmly jiggled my delicate nub, pulling another deep moan from my throat. The mouth at my throat growled, bit, growled, licked, and then bit again.

Two hands fondled my breasts. Two hands belonging to two different women. Someone was drawing on my belly, as well, and I wondered if there were somehow extra hands or mouths involved. *One of the hands I feel could be HIS*, I thought. The idea was incredibly hot. I had encountered him, made love to him, in dream space, but that is not quite the same as feeling a physical hand on my waking flesh. I shivered and felt an ache low in my body. The whine that escaped me was a plea for more.

Some shifting happened. The women rearranged themselves. Every hand and mouth moved, shifted to a new location, though one or two never left my body completely. As their fingertips trailed across my skin, I could feel the core of my spirit, the essence of my energetic being, like an effervescent bubbling of fine champagne just beneath my skin. I could see my spirit in my mind's eye, golden, shining, teeming with energy. The symbols were blazoned onto my being like neon signs, pulsating with energy.

The wheels of my chakras were spinning, the lotus flowers opening and sparkling as power coursed through them. As a talented and silky pair of lips explored my labia, I entered a vision of the jeweled lotus. It was like a kaleidoscopic hallucination, all light and energy and color flowing through my inner vision while physical delights poured through the funnel of my body.

Mouths and fingers stroked and licked my nipples. A hungry and searching mouth provided a feast of wet, deep kisses for my own.

Hands stroked and squeezed all of my skin. Nails punctuated my flesh in response to my moans and whimpers. Fingers found their way into my dew-slick tunnel. One, at first. Then a second, and then a third slender finger. Oh, Gods. Just the right amount of fullness to mimic a well-hung man's girth. My back arched and my body jerked in response, my knees widening instinctively. The fingers slid in and out of me, slowly. Deliberately. They let me get acclimated to the penetration before increasing their intensity.

I saw Robin in my mind. Only in my mind? No, I saw a dark shadow prowling our circle. But within my mind, I could see his throbbing erection. I could almost feel it. Almost taste it.

11

When the fingers inside me found and flicked my engorged g-spot, I felt a flood drench my thighs. My squeal of delight was high-pitched. An unsated sound. One that thanks the bringer of pleasure while asking for something more. Something deeper.

The fingers left me, and there was again a shift in the room. Someone new slid between my legs, her mouth eager, her hair brushing my damp thighs. Her fingers, as they entered me, were shorter and just a little thicker than the last. Her tongue sucked my lips, slowly licked my clit, and circled the opening that was filled with her own fingers. Then those fingers began to move. Oh, sweet Gods! The pulsating, swirling images overtook my mind, felt like multi-textured sensation throughout my whole body, my whole being. My legs pulled back even more, trying to create space within myself for the intense pleasure and power that coursed through me, up from my sex.

The energy in the room crackled and popped as I got closer to my own climax. Robin was there, hazy and indistinct in the thick smoke and candlelit gloom. He was just beyond the nest of writhing women. I was at its center, screaming as my covenmates squeezed and licked and kissed me closer to the brink. I held him in my sights, dim and fuzzy though he was, and focused all of my magical force on him. It was the energy I had raised, the energy we had all generated with wave after wave of orgasm building into a great column of unseen flame. I offered myself, body and soul, every ounce of energy, every drop of power to HIM. To bring him to me. To us. I saw him outside of our knot, but just as clearly, I felt him on top and inside of me, pumping, thrusting, kissing. As my body clenched, the other women channeled ALL of their energy through me, filling the cup that was my body and watching it overflow, sure of the goal, certain of my ability to see our work done. I screamed, "Robin!" in that final moment as pleasure and magical force overtook me, flooding me with ecstasy, ripping my own consciousness away, and granting absolute release.

I wavered and felt myself die for a moment. I lost track of my name, my purpose, my body. In the instant that followed, I wasn't even sure that I existed.

Every candle in the room had gone dark. My spirit seemed to settle back into my flesh, and I wiggled my toes. I remembered myself. My breathing was loud in my own ears, and I wondered if I sounded so loud to everyone else. They were all holding their breath.

I could feel Robin in the room, and I knew my sisters could feel him, too. We'd worked with enough spirits that a palpable presence was no impressive feat. Still, the question hung in the air. Had we accomplished manifestation? Was more than Robin's spiritual presence palpable?

Lilly fumbled with a lighter to reignite a candle. As she held it aloft, she searched the darkness for a form, but I knew exactly where I'd seen him. I pointed, and Lilly stretched her flame toward the corner. There, on one knee, sweating and panting as heavily as me, grinned Robin in the darkness.

Chapter 2

I'm not going to kid you. We made a fuss. We shrieked and hugged and high-fived each other as if we'd just won the lottery. Or just taken the gold in every event at the occult Olympics. It felt like that.

We seriously just manifested a corporeal spirit in our living room. Well, in a spare bedroom that had been converted into a temple room.

The only fact capable of keeping us grounded and even remotely humble was that we now all felt self-conscious and awkward. We knew what we wanted to say after the niceties were out of the way. I just had no clue which niceties even applied. *Thank you so much for coming. How was your trip?*

Um, no.

Evaline was the first to find her brain (and her voice). "Magister, how can we make you comfortable?"

He pushed himself to standing, and I could see it took some effort. "Food. Water. A chair, I think." I heard an accent in his voice, but I couldn't place it. British maybe, with something spicier behind it.

Pearl and Evaline moved to get refreshments. The bread and wine intended as our sacramental meal were on the other side of the room. Lilly headed to the kitchen for more substantial fare.

Grace ushered Robin to a chair, and just as he was about to sit, I noticed how very naked he was. "Wait!" I blurted. "Let me get you something." How had I not noticed he was so completely, wonderfully nude? I'd been staring at his bare torso since before he was even fully in the room with us.

I handed him the first bit of cloth that came into my hands, which happened to be an afghan crocheted by my grandma when I was a baby. Robin cocked an eyebrow at the green and yellow blanket but took it, wrapping it casually around his waist before sitting on the chair's cushion.

I shrugged. "Sorry. Habits. I don't usually let folks sit bare-assed on the furniture."

Grace laughed. "I'm sure you could make an exception for *him*. He isn't exactly *folks*."

I shrugged again. I wasn't ready to spend time pondering the great metaphysical question regarding the presence or absence of butt-crack sweat of a newly corporeal spirit. My instinct was to throw something washable under the bare bum before it landed on the upholstery. Done was done.

He winked at me, and my heart fluttered like a fucking fifteen-year-old. "This'll be fine for now."

The food was before us, and Lilly and Pearl performed our customary blessing.

"This is bread, the bounty of the fertile earth," Pearl said. "With my left hand, I take its life unto myself." She stabbed into the dark loaf with her red-handled knife.

Lilly held a cup of wine in her right hand, her own red knife in her left. "This is wine, joy of the earth. With my left hand, I cut its throat." She sliced her knife along the cup's wide opening.

In unison they said, "For what is truly taken is truly given." As they began to place the customary offering of bread and wine into a sacrificial bowl, I pointed out the obvious. "He's right here, ladies. The offering doesn't need to be symbolic. Give him his share by hand."

They blushed a little and held the wine and bread aloft for Robin to take. He reached toward the food and said, "And what is truly given is truly taken." He dipped the dark bread into the red wine and took a bloody bite.

"Here is shown a mystery," I added.

The sacraments passed to each of us, and we each ate and drank in turn. When they reached me, I dipped my finger into the

15

wine and marked bloody-looking crosses on my forehead, shoulders, and thighs.

Robin was watching us, a bare trace of a smile on his handsome face. I looked more closely at him as his eyes rested on my sisters. Was he actually handsome? Maybe. Or maybe it was power pouring out of him that made him so attractive. Perhaps if I saw this man, bereft of the intensity that now emanated from him, I would find him common. As he was, though, I could see nothing common about him. He was a miracle.

His dark hair curled in spirals past his shoulders. His skin was dusky. Was it sun-kissed or naturally dark? I had no idea. The only thing I could see clearly was that his amber eyes were rimmed with thick, dark lashes. He had that guy-liner look, but I knew his lash-line was all natural. Those eyes caught light like honey poured into deep pools. His eyes were anything but common. I was staring, and I only noticed that he was staring back when Grace cleared her throat.

"Give Rose some protein," she said. "She's having a hard time focusing."

I could feel the blush burning my cheeks. Maybe I was spacier than I thought.

Lilly brought me a slice of deli turkey and baby Swiss rolled into a tube and a Dixie cup full of roasted almonds. I nibbled my treats and avoided Robin's gaze, which I could feel was still on me.

"Well, I feel awkward," Pearl blurted. She had very little shame, our Pearl. She shrugged. "I do. I mean, what are we supposed to talk about now? Is it impolite to jump right into the reasons we brought Robin here?"

My face wasn't the only one stinging with heat now. My sisters looked uncomfortable, too.

"Oh, I know why I am here," Robin began.

Surprise is a lovely cure for bashfulness. "You do?" asked Pearl.

"Of course, he does," interjected Grace. "We've been working with him for years in our rituals. It stands to reason that he would know what is plaguing us."

"I should clarify," Robin corrected. "I know why I am here in the broadest sense. You are witches, and you have called me into this physical world to eliminate a threat that endangers you and other witches. What I don't know are the specifics of this threat. I remember vague hints of information, but it's like a dream that has barely stayed with me upon waking. In the past, it has taken a little time for me to have access to all my memories and power once I am corporeal. I imagine I'll need some rest before I am of any real help. In the meantime, perhaps Rose can explain it to me."

My head snapped up. "Why me? I mean, why me, specifically?"

"Yours is the voice that seems most familiar to me when I try to focus on this coven. You have acted as Maid more often than any other. And it is your voice that pleaded with me to come through the mists of time and space to be with you all."

Gulp. No pressure.

"Okay, well," I stammered as I tried to regain my composure. I actually really hated feeling like a teenager – on the spot and awkward. I let my irritation clear away that awkwardness. "We did call you to help us eliminate a threat. You have that part absolutely correct. The threat is a nasty preacher here in Indianapolis that is on a witch hunt. He's trying to make it illegal to practice witchcraft as a religion or as a craft."

"Dozens of our friends have been fined and had their businesses shut down in the last few months," Grace interjected. "Last week, one woman was arrested."

"On what grounds?" Robin asked. "Fraud?"

"No," Grace replied. "No, there has been too much proof in recent years that our arts are true for us to be called frauds."

"Well," Evaline added, "some of the so-called witches around town are frauds, and a few have been called to task to prove their skills. That was actually the beginning of the Registry."

17

"The Registry?" he echoed.

"Yeah," Evaline continued. "Dr. Sewall, the minister Rose mentioned, made a big push in the Indiana Legislature for all witches who make their living through the Craft to be listed on public record. If you're doing Tarot readings or witching for wells or selling spells, you have to get a license. It was called the Occult Practitioner Registration Act."

Pearl snort-laughed. "OPRA. Like the talk show lady. We thought it was a joke."

"A bad joke," said Lilly. "Most of us didn't register."

"Well, *most of us* didn't need to register," Grace added, the irritation evident in her voice. "*Most of us* weren't making a living as a witch."

Robin asked, already knowing the answer, "You were?"

She nodded. "I read Tarot cards and do psychic readings at a New Age shop on the south side. All the readers were required to register. Most of them are Christian, but they still had to register if they wanted to keep working. Only me and one other woman there are witches."

"I still think you should have quit and avoided the Registry," I said. It had been a sore point between us from the moment OPRA had hit media attention.

She worked hard not to roll her eyes, but the irritation was evident on her face. Both eyebrows were slightly arched and her full lips formed a tight line. She looked at me for a moment like she was going to say something pert, but she kept her silence. This was the look I got when I nagged Gracie. She knew I was right, though, so she didn't retort.

"You said Dr. Sewall?" Robin asked. "A *Sewall* was involved in the Salem trials. How long ago was that?"

"The Salem witch trials started in 1692," Grace replied, her momentary peevishness eclipsed by the opportunity to showcase her encyclopedic memory. "And yes, Samuel Sewall was an officer of the court."

Another snort from Pearl, the laughter derisive this time. "He's very proud of being the great-great-great-great-grand-cousin of that Puritan asshat, or whatever he says their relation is."

Robin's gaze hardened as he remembered the events of almost two and half centuries ago. "That court was a menace. They put nineteen people to death. They tried and convicted dozens more. Some died in prison. A few lucky ones escaped. Several were indicted but released on bond. You want no part of that happening again." He sat for another moment before adding. "Or worse. The trials in Germany, England, and Ireland were so much more devastating to our bloodlines."

The grief and anxiety on Robin's face hurt my heart. "We've been told by more recent historians that most of the women and men executed for witchcraft were not truly witches. Is that false?"

A fire burned in his eyes as he thought back to the fires that claimed so many lives. "Most of the people brought to trial were not witches, no. Many were, though, and I lost several beloved daughters, lovers, and sisters in those dark years." He fixed his hard gaze on me for the beat of a breath, then softened and said, "I lost my wife."

I held his eye contact, and I knew I was holding a deep pain. *His wife?* I didn't know he had a wife. Curiosity nearly overcame compassion, but I managed to bookmark my questions for a less raw interview.

"You were right to bring me," he said, looking away from me. "We must set the situation to rights, as swiftly and silently as we can manage. This Sewall is likely to be as dangerous as the last one that set his hand to exterminating witches. I'd rather we give him no opportunity to make any real progress toward his goals."

Pearl shifted her weight on her cushion, rolling her shoulders to relieve tension from her neck and back. "Let's not get panicked, though. Our Rev. Sewall may be an asshat, but I don't think he is trying to kill us. He's just making our lives difficult. Fines and registries and whatnot aren't as big and bad as witch trials and executions."

Evaline nodded her agreement, while Grace said nothing and looked noncommittally at a ring with a green stone on her finger.

It was Lilly who spoke next. "These things always start somewhere. How many holocausts do we have to have before we see the pattern?"

"Grace did a reading last month which told us to prepare for battle," I said. "We've done several since then, including one in which we called on you, Robin, as an oracle. Do you remember?"

He tilted his head and squinted his eyes, as if trying to make the memory shake loose and rattle its way to the front of his brain. "Maybe. I remember seeing all of you, and I remember that it was recent. I see fire and violence now, as I try to recall the conversation. But, no, I can't bring up the specific details yet."

"You said we were to be attacked on two fronts," I continued. "One from without and one from within the Craft."

He nodded, and when he spoke again, his eyes were unfocused. "A dark and wicked eye will soon light upon this coven, and it will seek to destroy you by means of your worldly persecutors."

I set my jaw and dared Evaline or the others to disagree with me. "We cannot take this lightly. We must ready ourselves for whatever is coming."

Chapter 3

First on our battle preparation plan was getting Robin up to full strength. A centuries-old magister with memory fog and weak muscles wasn't going to be of much use to us. We needed him ready and primed, whatever that meant.

We didn't know what he would be like at full strength, so we weren't sure how to get him there. Nothing like having a strategy before starting an endeavor! For the moment, we agreed to take turns caring for him in our homes. He would have to let us know when he felt ready to proceed.

Gracie and I kept him at our place first. He was already on the premises, after all, since the temple room for the coven was in the house Grace and I shared in the tiny suburb of Monrovia, southwest of Indy.

We'd lived here for about five years, so far. Neither of us were native to this specific area, and we didn't know many local people. Our social and work lives revolved around Indianapolis, but the commute wasn't bad, being on I-70 like we were.

The town itself was cute. Not even big enough for its own stoplight, we had an IGA, a mom-and-pop gas station that the locals call "Bible's" despite the Bible family having sold it to a Pakistani man well before we moved to town, and a Dollar General. The Love's truck stop, which was newer to town than Grace and me, brought a McDonald's and a Subway. The post office was run by a friendly blond woman who closed shop every day by 3:30pm, and the hair salon was just the sort of gossip hub you would expect.

I'm not sure our neighbors even knew we existed. We lived a few miles outside the thicket of houses that actually made up the town. Three or four miles in any direction brought you to areas that the residents called by different town names. Hall. Wilbur. Of course, these settlements didn't retain any of the features that meant "town" in my mind. A collection of ten houses with a church or an old schoolhouse that was now considered a local landmark. I couldn't even consider that a subdivision, let alone a town.

They certainly didn't know that two witches lived side by side with them, although I think our nearest neighbor suspected that two lesbians might be in residence. She wasn't wrong there. Grace and I were both attracted to women, Grace a little more so than me. We were not a couple, though, as the neighbor lady believed. We'd tried being lovers and failed. No sexual chemistry. Very disappointing. Still, we were best friends, and we shared a life together much like we would have done if we were in a committed romantic relationship.

Robin's first few days, then, were spent in our witch cottage in the woods.

"Your home is lovely," he said on his first morning with us.

What a mundane beginning to a chat with an otherworldly spirit! I laughed a little at the absurdity of the situation.

He winked. "I always notice what is lovely and wild in a place."

I looked around our little unkempt yard. I loved my herbs and let them run roughshod over the grass and into the trees. I hated grassy lawns, and I was a miserable keeper of the tidy grassy patches that were required in subdivisions. Grace was less inclined to mow and weed than I was. I adored the spreading lemon balm and gave dandelions no reason to worry about extermination at my hands. I'm sure the neighbor lady disapproved of the messy rose bushes, lavender, and Queen Anne's lace that bordered the edges of our space. I'm equally sure that I didn't care.

I walked with Robin that morning through my messy garden and into the woods. A dozen honey bees danced on the tops of the tall plants, and I smiled at their happy work. Robin watched me, saying nothing.

We sat under a hickory grove at the edge of woods, the buzzing of the yellow sisters bringing a sleepy calm to the warm morning. I watched the sunlight pour over the green world in front of us and felt the cool green shade above and behind us. I do so love the woods.

Robin sprawled back on the mossy ground and sang. The melody was like a lullaby to me, soft and mournful. The lyrics slipped through my mind like honey sliding off a spoon. Some stuck, while the rest poured heavily away into a sweet pool. As he sang, my mind wandered, and I had a vision of gnomes laboring industriously around me in the woods, their brown and green heads bobbing above the grasses and weeds. Energy flowed like a river along the dragon lines under the earth. Dark eyes watched from the green shade as we lay in the dappled sunlight.

Robin moved his hands in a wide arc along the ground, and red capped toadstools emerged in a circle around us. "A fairy circle," he said simply.

"You're getting stronger already, I see," I said. The magic he had done with a wave of his hand was a magic I knew, though I admit it was a much more challenging task for me than it had been for him.

"Sitting on the earth makes it easier," he replied.

"Is your memory returning, as well?" I asked.

"A bit," he said. He leaned closer to me, an intensity in his face. "I remember you."

A chill ran down my spine. I'd had a relationship with him in a spiritual sense for years. I would have been embarrassed and anguished if he hadn't known me now. I blushed as I thought of the encounters I could recall. Others might only understand these moments as fantasies, the nights I spent with my spirit lover. To me, though, they had been as real as he was now, lying with me under the trees of my back yard.

"What do you recall?" I asked, breathless.

He reached across the small expanse that separated us and brushed a stray auburn strand from my face. His hand traced spirals down my arm, ending at my hand. He pointed to the moldavite ring I wore, its green glass the result of a meteorite striking a sandy spot in Europe thousands of years ago. "I know that under this ring is a small tattoo that I told you to get."

I held my breath. "Why did you tell me to get it?"

He scooted his muscular frame closer to me, the intensity never leaving his eyes. I could feel the energy of his body where it nearly touched mine. It was electricity, and my body responded with thrills like fine champagne bubbles under my skin. He leaned close to my face, never breaking eye contact. "Because you're mine, lovely Rose. I love and cherish you. I have known you since you were a child, and I see in you the spirit of my beloved, born through the ages as a queen of witches."

This was not the first time he had shared his love of me, but it was the first time I had ever heard it spoken aloud. He had come to me in dreams, fantasies, and spiritual encounters since I was young. Our relationship hadn't started as a love affair. No, he had come first as a mentor, a friend, a wise teacher. As I matured, though, our relationship changed. By the time I was having my first sexual relationships with physical partners, I was also having intense and vivid encounters with Robin.

Of course, I felt insane. I was fantasizing about the devil coming to me, seducing me, pleasuring me. He looked like the devil, at least. He looked like Tim Curry in *Legend*, all red skin and bull horns. He was taboo. He was hot.

I knew then that I was a different sort of girl. I had been raised to hate and fear this image, and instead I was drawn to it. I didn't want to murder babies or treat people like trash. Truthfully, I didn't think that had much to do with him. He felt like sex, like the ultimate in sexual energy, like everything a good girl isn't supposed to want but still does.

Years passed before I found my first teachers within the Craft. The Arts may be more public than they had been in years past, but they were still underground, hidden, occult. Popular publishers were spewing books on Wicca and Neo-Paganism, and

I read all I could of these. Like gorging on sweets, though, they didn't satisfy. I knew there was more. I kept looking until I found a real teacher. Until one found me.

Witchcraft isn't inherited. Well, it isn't entirely inherited. Television and movies want you to believe that only certain bloodlines have power. Not true. Your blood and body have power all on their own. Your brain is a much more magical tool than any wand or dagger or robe. Still, some families have passed the Art along their lineage in more potent concentrations than others.

There are other witches in my family, even in my own generation. I have a fifth cousin in Arkansas with the blood. As heritage goes, though, my family isn't one of the well-known witch families. I can't trace my lineage back to Salem, though I have found tentative links between my family line and that of Dame Alice Kyteler. As witchcraft royalty goes, she's high on the list. She was the first Irish woman convicted of witchcraft during the infamous witch trials. A noblewoman. It is through her and her coven that Robin son of Art enters the trial records. Robin Artisson, who was lying on the mossy forest floor with me now.

"Do you still see me as the red devil of your young adulthood, my Rose?" he said, a grin on his face. He already knew the answer.

"Sometimes," I admitted. "Rarely. That image doesn't frighten me anymore, and I don't find it particularly taboo these days."

"I'm glad you grew to see me in many forms," he said.

Our conversation wasn't sexual at all. Why was my body responding as if it were? My gods, I was horny. Is that inelegant to say? It doesn't matter. It's what I was.

I studied his eyes. Such thick lashes. I would have loved to have lashes like that.

He touched my face again, this time caressing a cheek. His hand reached for the nape of my neck, and his fingers twisted into the red curls there. A thrill ran through my whole body. Danger, lust. I'm not much into domination and submission, but I do like it when a partner isn't shy about their desires. Robin wanted me. I could feel it. And I wanted him so badly that I was sure every blade of grass and every leaf within a mile radius must be able to feel it. My body thrummed with the electricity of his touch.

He pulled me into a kiss, and a lightning bolt of energy zipped through my core, igniting my sex into a wet flame. I was flooded, almost embarrassingly so. I leaned all the way back into the moss and let him cover my torso with his own.

My breasts strained against his toned chest, trying to touch him with every soft bit of my skin as his mouth consumed me. I drank him down, too, feeling the honeyed flow of energy between us. His hand reached for my breast, and I felt a shock of power as our heart chakras connected. His other forearm was braced above my head, holding his torso easily above me while his knee came to rest between my own. I could feel his thigh, muscled and powerful, between my own. My pelvis curled toward him in an instinctive effort to get closer. In a quick and fluid movement, his hips pressed against me and away again. Shockwaves of desire and energy flooded my body from my sex up to my heart.

I was becoming delirious in my ecstasy and desire. Emotion burned the backs of my eyes, and I wanted to weep for joy at finally having Robin in my arms. Spiritual sex with him had been mind-blowing and intimate. Having him here in the flesh was overwhelmingly delightful. Time seemed to stop, and the whole universe was swirling inside my body and mind.

Lifting himself above me, he tore off the tight-fitting t-shirt I had loaned him. His body was far too masculine for my clothes. Looking at his naked chest was a rapture all of its own. His amber eyes glowed with a primal fire as he watched me looking at him. I longed to run my hands over his smooth, dark skin and feel the brush of his silky chest hair under my palms. That amazing chest was just out of reach, though, and I was enjoying the view. Sometimes we need to let one sense really revel in the pleasure of its sensation before adding another into the mix. Yes, I wanted to touch him, taste him, smell him close to me. But it could wait a moment.

I arched my back and pulled my own shirt off without lifting myself off the ground. It was a sinuous, serpentine sort of action, and I felt like a snake shedding her skin. I could picture myself as Robin saw me, auburn curls and pale skin aglow in the emerald grass. I felt the energy building between us, each drinking in the vision of the other. A snippet of Shakespeare flashed in my mind – Juliet saying, "I'll look to like, if looking liking move." Looking at Robin, framed by the forest and crowned by the sun, moved me beyond liking, beyond the lust that I had always felt for him.

He threw back his head and laughed, the pleasure of the moment overtaking him. He stood, pulling me to my feet and holding me tight to his body with one arm encircling me. The other hand stroked my curls, cradled my head, and pulled me into another soul-stirring kiss. My arms snaked around his neck, and we swayed, almost dancing.

I withdrew first. My body was overflowing with the magic of this passion, and the roil of energy pushed me to impatience. I need a long, slow climb to the heights of sexual ecstasy, but I didn't think I could stand to have our bodies separate for even another minute. I would take the time for languorous lovemaking and extended foreplay, just maybe not this time. Today, right now, I wanted to connect with Robin bodily, completely, immediately.

I kissed his chest and belly as I slid down his body, taking the soft, drawstring pants with me. He stepped out of the cotton and kicked it to the side. I stood, giving the head of his cock a quick flick of my tongue as I went. I heard the sharp intake of his breath at this fleeting touch, and I kissed him deeply again as I stood on tiptoe to reach his lips. His hands skimmed my waist and gripped the curve of my hips, almost clawing at the denim of my jeans as he circled the band looking for the fastener. I could feel a frustration in his fingertips, and I thought for a moment that he might rip the jeans open. I lowered my hands to the button and unzipped myself.

He mimicked me, easing himself to his knees in front of me, pulling my jeans and panties away from my hips as he went. I shimmied to free the denim from around my knees and flicked it to the side.

Robin knelt in front of me for a moment, not moving. I was about to join him down in the grass again when he suddenly curled one arm between my knees, pulling my leg over his shoulder. His hands moved to brace me, one on my leg, one on my ass, while he moved his head between my thighs. He nibbled the thigh that rested on his shoulder, and then he licked. And then he moved. He kissed my vulva, his wet tongue gliding sensuously across my labia, searching for the sweet water of my sex. I moaned and tried to move my leg away from his shoulder. I didn't particularly want foreplay. I was already so aroused, I just wanted him inside me. But my attempt to move was in vain. His hands held me in place, and my efforts only served to position my cunt more directly into his eager mouth. He licked and sucked and flicked my rapidly swelling lips and clit, making me even wetter than I had already been.

Insane from the pleasure of his mouth and unsteady from my stance, I could take no more. I grabbed his hair by the fistfuls in both hands and pulled his head back, forcing him to stop and look up at me. His eyes swam in their lusty intoxication. He blinked twice before focusing on my face.

"I need you inside me," I said. "I have to feel you in me. Now." He grinned up at me, my juices glistening on his lips and goatee. "Please," I added.

"I would be delighted to please you," he said. He slid two fingers along the slit of my yoni before he fully released my leg, sending an aching shiver from my cunt through my torso.

I sat in front of him, feet planted on either side of him, not modest in the slightest about being splayed open before him. My hand reached out for his throbbing cock, gratified and grateful for the thickness and weight of it in my palm. I leaned back, gently pulling him toward me until our mouths locked in another sensuous kiss as I reclined again in the grass. My legs hitched back automatically, fully presenting myself to him, ready to welcome him into me. The head of his cock slid across my slick opening, and he reached down to guide himself home.

The feeling of him entering me for the first time was unbearably pleasant. He was full and thick, and he filled me up completely. My whole body felt like one nerve, with my sex as the nucleus, the center. The sensation of him filling me, the tip of his penis just grazing my cervix, his pubic bone pushed fully against my clit, sent a flood of joy and pleasure through my entire being. I gushed around him in an unexpected orgasm. Wet as it was, it was only a little orgasm, and I was far from finished.

He grinned and growled at my flood, and then he began to move inside me. With each long pull out and away from me, I could feel my body holding him tight. And as he pushed home again each time, my clit and labia sent electric flashes through my whole being.

I'd never felt anything like this before. I'd had plenty of sex with enough lovers to know what I liked. I knew what a broad spectrum of pleasure could be found in the bed of different men and women. But never, ever, had I experienced the sort of biochemical, electromagnetic, cosmic reactions that I was feeling under this man. It felt like a switch had been turned on, sending electrical signals to nerves I'd never felt before. The feeling like champagne under my skin that I had felt in the summoning ritual returned, stronger this time. I had never felt that sensation before last night, and a part of me knew that it was Robin's touch I was feeling in the ritual. He had activated something in me, though what it was, I didn't know. Perhaps only a deeper carnal knowledge. Perhaps something more potent.

My moans were loud and ragged. Each thrust brought some vocal response from me. His breath on my neck and breasts as he pumped in and out of me, the occasional grunt or growl of pleasure as a wave of delight hit him, was working a special magic on me. I could feel the orgasm building, and I knew it wouldn't be long before it overtook me. This was so fast for me. I never came quickly, and the knowledge that Robin was so in touch with me that he could pull two orgasms from my body in such a short amount of time made me squirm.

"You going to come for me, sweet girl?" he purred in my ear.

I nodded and held him tight, pulling him as close to my flesh as I could.

"You ready?" he asked.

I could only respond in a wail of delight, my hands gripping his ass as he thrust hard and fast.

"Do you want me to come with you?"

"Oh gods, yes," I nodded.

"Inside you?" he breathed.

I started to nod, but it no longer mattered. I had gone over the edge, and I pulled him with me. Wave after wave of orgasm broke through my body, Robin's eyes turning wild as he bellowed and filled me with his liquid heat. We rocked through the spasms of delight, convulsing as the pleasure echoed through our flesh.

We fell away from each other, panting and laughing into the soft grass. I rolled my head to the side, aware of colors under the shade that I hadn't seen before. Outside the circle of mushrooms that Robin had called up earlier was another circle, this one of flowers, riotous in their many bright colors.

"Did you do that?" I asked him, the awe evident in my breathless voice.

"No, my love," he said. "You did."

Chapter 4

"No!" the man pleaded. "No, I beg of you. Don't do this."

A red rag stained with oil and dirt was stuffed into his mouth as he cried.

"Your screams will not help you escape, nor will they help us achieve our task," said the woman's voice. He couldn't see her face under the crimson robe she wore. The eye holes cut into her hood were uncanny, and the man shuddered at her brief touch. She withdrew her scarlet gloved hand and drew one finger toward the place where her mouth would be. "Suffer in silence, lest your suffering be multiplied."

His body trembled, and he couldn't suppress the occasional whines of terror that spasmed out of his throat. Why was this happening? *What* was happening? He'd been drugged or something. That wouldn't have been so bad. After all, he had been in the neighborhood that locals call "Sudden Death" looking for a score. There were a few abandoned houses and unrented apartments that were easy to squat in for the night or the week, and the drugs might as well have been peddled by ice cream vendors, they were so open and accessible.

A woman in a red dress had been cruising the block he was on. He'd taken her for a hooker. He figured she'd know where to find who was slinging at this godforsaken hour. She had offered him a taste of what she used, something in an eyedropper. She'd put a couple of drops in his nostril and then walked away smiling like that cat who ate the canary everyone talks about. The world turned into a happy blur of sodium lamps and trailing car lights. He felt like he was flying. This was good shit. He'd have to find this hooker again. If all her shit was so good, he'd take a little of everything she offered.

The flying changed to falling. That repeated falling where you jerk and know you're already on the ground, but you keep feeling like a stool got kicked out from under you. His head hurt now, and the points of candlelight around the dark room were like daggers in his eyes.

Why was he tied down? His arms and legs were pulled away from his torso by tense ropes. The bitch that stuffed the rag in his mouth must be the same one who dosed him. What had she looked like? He hadn't even noticed her face on the street, only that red dress hugging a plump rump and the magic bottle in her hands.

There was movement in the room. He could hear other feet shuffling over the grimy concrete floor, but the woman in red was the only one he could see. She was still blurry to him, a dark, smeared light in a darker cavern.

The room was so dim that he couldn't see the walls in the flickering candlelight. There seemed to be nothing in the room beyond the circle of light emitted by the four tapers. One was at his feet, another at his head, and the last two were placed to each side of him. Something like red paint was smeared on the ground around him, making strange symbols around his star-shaped body.

Part of his brain wanted to laugh at how stereotypically Satanic the scene was. It was like something out of a death metal video or an 80's horror flick. Mostly, though, he was terrified. He didn't think he was the non-consenting star in a music video. He was pretty sure this crazy red bitch was going to slice him up.

She returned with a brass bowl swinging from long chains. Something was smoking inside it. She chanted as she swung the fumes in wide circles, walking counterclockwise around his body sprawled on the floor.

The words were Latin or something. He couldn't understand what she was saying. Some words were familiar, recalled from his Catholic childhood. *Sanctus. Venire. Ave.* It sounded like a prayer, but words like *diabolus* and *satanas* raised the hairs on his arms and the bile to his gut. He wasn't a religious man.

Hadn't been to church since he was a young teen. But this, this was a travesty of what he had known.

Male voices were chanting in the darkness. Two of them, he thought. One was high and nasal, the other low and thick-tongued. Neither had the grace or power of the woman, although her grace was like a snake – venomous and sinister.

Yes, he could see them now. Black robes like her red one. Same hoods with the creepy eye holes. Black gloves. She sprinkled black dirt now as she circled, still chanting the same words. *"Sanctus Satanas, sanctus."* She made sure to drop dirt on his head, hands, and feet.

Next, she circled him with a bowl. He felt thick, wet drops of liquid hit his face. He saw red droplets on his hands. Blood. Of course.

Her final path around him featured fire. She swung some sort of flaming ball from a long chain. He could smell the fuel, like lighter fluid. She grazed him with the fire's tongue as she made this last circle, her chant now a gloating hymn.

She touched the flame ball to the floor and a slick oil that he hadn't known encircled him caught fire. Panic was rising inside him. Oh, sweet Jesus! Please don't let them burn me! Please don't!

"I told you not to speak," she said harshly. "Your shrieks are irksome, although your fear adds to the power of our rite."

The three robed figures took positions around him in an equilateral triangle. She was at his head, they were nearer to his knees.

"We come to the Templum Inferni to open the portal that a dark king might walk among us," she said.

"Fientes ostium," they chanted quietly as she spoke.

"We bring this sacrifice as an offering to the gate keepers," she said. "May his flowing blood bring you life, his last breath bring you vitality."

"Aperite portam," the chant changed.

"With this first gift of life, we open the gates and make ready the road of our king!"

"Parate viam."

She knelt, a knife in her hands. Leaning across his shoulder, she traced the sigil of the demon she sought onto her victim's chest. He writhed and shrieked in agony. Laughing and triumphant, she plunged her dagger into the bloody symbol, sliding neatly between his ribs. He choked on his blood, and the world went dark.

Chapter 5

A few days later, Evaline brought us coffee and bad news.

"Rose?" she called from the living room after letting herself in. We never locked our doors, and our coven sisters knew it. They were the only visitors we had, and they were family. We had warded the place against entry from others. That was a simple magic. An unwelcome or unknown person standing on our front porch would not be able to enter the house without explicit invitation. If they dared to try the knob, it would catch as if it were physically locked. An intruder attempting entry through a window would meet even more resistance. None had tried it yet. I would almost have felt sorry for anyone who dared. Almost.

"Grace, are you guys up?" she tried again.

I heard Grace startle in her bed. She was a sound sleeper. Any effort to wake her produced a sound of alarm.

"I'm coming," I slurred through my sleep-numb mouth. Robin rolled out of bed at the same time. I tied a green silk robe around my naked self, while he pulled on a pair of pajama pants I'd loaned him. We still needed to take him shopping soon. Poor man had no clothes. Not that I was complaining about that.

"Be right there. Lemme pee first," I followed up.

My morning ritual being curtailed, I hit the basics. Tinkle, toothbrush, and top knot. My hair was a wild red mess in the morning, so a sloppy bun was as good as it would get in the few seconds I felt I had to devote to my appearance.

Stumbling a little less than before, I made my way into the living room. Evaline was already turning on the tv, fighting with the remote control to find the channel she wanted.

She handed me a creamy, candy-flavored latte and pointed at the screen. "You're not going to believe this shit," she said, and she turned up the volume on a report already in progress.

"*... this horrific and grisly murder. Rev. Sewall and his congregation at Guardians of Faith Ministry have assembled in front of the Indianapolis Metropolitan Police Headquarters, demanding that the perpetrator of this heinous crime be brought to justice.*"

The camera cut away from the dour but pretty brunette woman with the Channel 13 microphone to show a frowning man in his mid-fifties, dark hair gone silver at the temples, wearing a black three piece suit. A scrolling ticker tape message at the bottom of the screen announced that Dr. Thomas Sewall was calling for justice in the ritual murder of a homeless man. He held a black Bible in his hands that he shook and pointed as visual punctuation to his speech.

"*This atrocity cannot be allowed to stand. The markings on this piteous, indigent man's body clearly show that it was a ritual murder. We've been working to eradicate the blight of witchcraft from our city, and this is an act of retaliation. If we, the good people of Indianapolis, do nothing and allow the perpetrator of this heinous act to go undiscovered and unpunished, more atrocities and horrors will befall us. All religions of the Light have a hatred of witchcraft, from Christianity to Islam, from Buddhism to Hinduism. All people of piety and faith shun the darkness of witchcraft and Devil worship.*"

His sermon continued, no doubt, but the camera returned its focus to the brunette reporter.

"*So far, we have no official word from the Indianapolis Metropolitan Police about the murder that took place on Indy's east side last night. Several media outlets received a gruesome picture from an anonymous source showing the body of the murder victim, which had been mutilated and carved with ritualistic symbols. The graphic nature of the photograph prevents us from airing it, but we can show two related images that we hope will bring this ritual assailant to justice.*"

The screen now displayed a sigil, shown in black and white. It was the symbol of a demon listed in the *Ars Goetia, the Lesser Key of Solomon*. The symbol dated back to magical practice in the Middle Ages, at least, though some magicians claimed it could be traced all the way back to King Solomon himself. Rumor has it that Solomon built his great temple in Jerusalem with the aid of 72 demons whom he trapped and controlled.

"*This symbol was part of the markings left on the man's torso. Authorities believe it is connected to a demon who is often worshiped by witches and Satanists. According to one expert, this demon represents the very worst of human attributes and the vilest of intentions. Witches seeking to harm their neighbors and gain unholy powers have called upon him for patronage across the centuries.*"

A second image now appeared on the screen. The blurry, enlarged image of a seemingly female figure in a red hooded cloak now dominated the screen. The figure's face was completely hidden behind the rounded hood, but the symbol of a bindrune was evident upon the torso of her robe. Long, dishwater blond hair spilled past her shoulders and onto her satin-covered breasts. She held a knife in one hand, its wavy blade pointing skyward, while her other hand made the sign of the horns.

"*This is a detail of the picture that was sent to media outlets early this morning. This is the same picture that shows the mutilated body of an unidentified man. We can only...*"

The reporter's voice stopped for a moment, evidently interrupted by a producer at the other end of her ear piece. When she resumed speaking, she was clearly on the move, her breath panting slightly into her microphone.

"*Indianapolis Police Chief Marshall Vance is preparing to make a statement here in front of the headquarters. This is the first public statement made by police officials regarding last night's grisly ritual murder.*"

The reporter and her cameraman got to the Police Chief's position on the front steps just in time for him to start speaking. She thrust her microphone toward him. He was reading from a typed piece of paper, not looking at the cameras or the assembled crowd.

"At 4:34 AM, the Indianapolis Metropolitan Police Department, along with several other state and federal agencies and a number of media organizations, received an emailed photograph from an unidentified source depicting a slain male, approximately thirty-five years old, and a person wearing robes, whom we assume to be female. The only other information provided in the email message with this image was an address, located on the city's east side, near the 3700 block of Post Road. Officers arriving on the scene found the deceased, as pictured. We have identified the man, whom we believe to have been homeless for the last several years, and are attempting to contact his next of kin before releasing his name. A full investigation is now underway to identify the person or persons responsible for his murder. We ask that anybody with information about this crime please come forward. Thank you."

A cacophony of shouted questions followed Chief Vance as he turned and re-entered the building, a wall of officers holding the reporters on the grounds in front of the steps.

I looked at Grace, who was sitting ramrod straight on the edge of her favorite wing-backed chair. She was trembling and pale.

"Click it off," I said to Evaline as the reporter on the screen began her recap of the police chief's message. "Are you okay, Gracie?" I asked.

She nodded in an uncertain staccato rhythm., saying nothing. "Would you like some skullcap tea to calm your nerves?" Another nod.

Robin moved to sit beside her while I bustled off to the adjoining kitchen to brew her cup. Skullcap wasn't tasty, but it was a great sedative.

"What a way to wake up on a Saturday morning," I said from the sink, competing with the running water for volume.

"This is a real problem," Evaline responded. "This could be devastating."

"I know," I said. "Did you see those symbols? They're right about whose sigil that is, you know." I would not say the demon's name. Despite what the reporter had shared, most witches did not, in fact call upon that nasty spirit for help. He was a bad piece of work, and I didn't want to call his attention to our coven by speaking his name aloud. In fact, I found it worrisome that we were now going to have dozens of reporters repeating it on their newscasts multiple times each day. It would be like a mantra or a prayer, sending energy to the spirit from all over the city as people repeated it in tones of awe and horror.

"I know," Evaline said, her voice sounding tight. "I wish they wouldn't have kept saying his name again and again like that." Her thoughts echoed my own. "And did you see the symbol on the woman's robes."

"It was a bindrune, I believe," I said.

"Yeah," she agreed. "It's so strange, though. That bindrune is for protection, if I remember correctly. It doesn't make sense that it would be on that robe. Not in that sort of ritual."

Something was bothering me about the symbol. I'd seen it recently, in some other context. The circumstances were just beyond the reach of my memory, though. When and where had I seen it? My need to remember felt urgent, and I was frustrated that I couldn't call up the whole memory.

"We should call Lilly and Pearl over. Maybe we could do some magic to bring the murderer to justice before the city starts a witch hunt in earnest," Evaline suggested. "That murder was clearly done by someone who is connected to the Craft. Someone very, very dark."

"We probably should do something," I agreed.

Grace spoke up, shaking but firm. "I want no part of it," she said.

I scooped the herbs into a tea-ball and waited for the pot to boil. "What do you mean?" I asked. "This affects us. We should act."

"It might," Grace said. "And it might not. I think we shouldn't create an energetic bond with what is happening. If we do magic to affect the outcome of the investigation, we are entangling ourselves in that outcome. I don't want that. Not for me, and not for any of you."

"Okay," said Evaline. "I see what you are saying, but I think we should talk about it as a coven."

"I don't want to talk about it," Grace replied, her voice strained and tears filling her eyes. "Just watching that news report ..." She couldn't finish her sentence, as emotion overtook her. She held her breath, trying to regain her composure. "I think we would be safer," she began, her breath still held tight. "I don't..." she was stammering now. She gulped for air and hyperventilation overtook her. "I ... don't ... want ... want ... to ...." It was no use. Her breathing was now obviously painful, her face red and wet from her failed attempts at controlling her voice.

Robin scooped her into his lap, tucking her head to his broad chest. "Ssshhhh," he whispered. He rocked her like a child, held tight in his arms.

Evaline sat frozen in her seat. We had seen Grace have a panic attack before, and none of us were particularly good at helping her through the process. Evaline was the best of us, perhaps. The most naturally compassionate and patient. Pearl was a talented healer of physical ailments, but she was as easily overwhelmed by other people's emotions as Lilly and I were.

The spout on the teapot whistled for attention, and Grace jumped. I pulled the pot off the stove and poured the steaming water over the tea-ball. It was Grace's favorite cup, although I now suspected she was too far gone in her panic attack to notice. The brew needed to steep for a few minutes to be potent enough to help Grace's raw nerves. I readied an ice cube to cool the tea down fast and raw honey to mellow the taste.

"Ssshhhh," he continued to purr into her ear as she sobbed on his shoulder. Her whole body was shaking, and he rocked her while stroking her hair. "It's okay, little sister," he said softly. "It will be okay. I'm here."

Several minutes passed, and I set Grace's steaming tea cup on the end table next to her chair. She looked at it, but made no move to take it. Her eyes were unfocused, and her breathing was coming steadier.

"That's it," Robin cooed. "Just let it pass. Would you like your tea now, sweet girl?"

She nodded feebly. He lifted the cup and held it to his lips, blowing the steam away from the surface of the liquid. She took it in her hands and lowered the cup to her lap. She looked weak and forlorn. He nudged the cup to her lips, where she finally sipped it.

"Ugh," she complained. "I hate this stuff."

"Take your medicine, little sister," he prodded. "You will feel better for it."

She continued to blow on the hot brew, sipping occasionally, as the shuddering subsided in her body. We all sat in silence, listening to Grace's ragged breathing regain a normal flow. I stared at the carpet, and Evaline seemed to be looking obliquely at a painting on the wall.

"Do you remember when I first held you?" Robin asked Grace. She paused before nodding, the childish little nod of a young girl seeking approval and fearing a reprimand. I'd seen these little girl mannerisms from her before, most often following emotional turmoil. Grace's childhood was a dark place, filled with rebuke and abuse. Psychological upset made her as vulnerable and immature as she was during those early years, I think.

"Tell me about it," he said.

She paused again, hesitant about beginning. "I was about nine. I had been reading a book about the Greek gods," she said. "I was particularly drawn to Apollo, and so I prayed to the sun every morning as it rose. I asked for my sight to be taken and replaced with the Second Sight, as I had read in one of the tales. I stared hard into the bright sun every day as I prayed." A breath shuddered through her.

"I came to you as a golden man, clothed in the radiance of the sun," Robin said. "Do you recall?"

She nodded, her affirmation stronger this time. "You held me then, just like you are holding me now." She snuggled into his shoulder, the cup half-finished in her hands.

"Yours was a true sacrifice, and it was repaid with the Sight you desired," he said.

"I got my first pair of glasses that same year," she said. "My eyes went bad fast."

"And I told you then that I would always care for you," he said. "My little sister." He continued to rock her, and her eyes closed. I took the cup from her hands, and Robin carried Grace to her bed.

With Grace out of the room, Evaline looked at me again and spoke low. "This is more upsetting for her than I would think. I mean, it's a big deal, but we need to take care of it and not lose our heads."

I shrugged. "It might pass," I said. "You never know with Grace. We'll do what we think is right, and if she changes her mind, she can join us when she feels ready."

We made plans to gather the necessary ingredients and meet back at my house as soon as possible. Evaline would go to her favorite metaphysical shop for supplies. I would coordinate times with Lilly and Pearl.

I said a little internal prayer of thanks that the moon was waning. This work would be easier under a waning moon.

Chapter 6

My job is neither witchy nor exciting. I think people have the mistaken impression that every witch does inherently witchy work. They believe we are all spell-casters, energy healers, and card readers. They think that we curse one unhappy neighbor on behalf of another or that we make the hunk fall in love with the desperate cat lady in his apartment building.

Some of us are certainly gifted healers, like Pearl. Others are indeed talented psychics, like Grace. Those skills are marketable in ways that necromancy, weather magic, and shapeshifting will never be. Those are economic realities.

My insurance industry skills would never place me on some horrendous watch list, though. I have been grateful for the anonymity that my day job provides. I worry about Grace having her name on the stupid OPRA rolls. They reminded me of the Indian Rolls from which some of my own ancestors had deftly avoided inclusion. Worse yet, they reminded me of the sorts of lists that included the names of Jewish and Romany families in Nazi Germany. My Choctaw ancestors may have avoided the Indian rolls, but some of Lilly's gypsy forbears hadn't been so lucky. It has never been a good thing to have your name included on a list because you were different. This newest list couldn't be any better than its many predecessors.

Being an insurance claims processor isn't sexy, but it keeps me off lists of the unfavorable sort. I don't try to live inside the broom closet, but I haven't found a good reason to broadcast my witchcraft affiliations, either. My co-workers seem to think I am a hippy, what with my herbal teas and the fact that I have been caught doing yoga in an unused conference room during my lunch break.

The lady in the cubicle next to mine seems to disapprove of these little New Age nuances. She was the one who walked in on me doing yoga. You would have thought she caught me masturbating in there. She could barely gasp out the words, "Pardon me," before backtracking out of the room and snapping the door closed. I had been worried that I had actually violated some sort of company policy. She was even more of a "rules lawyer" than I was. A quick check with my boss set me at ease, though. As long as I checked the room sign-up to make sure a meeting wasn't slotted for that space, I was free to stretch and meditate in there during lunch.

My cubicle neighbor never truly recovered her composure around me, though. She never made eye contact with me, and I had seen her talking about me to a pinch-faced woman in another nearby cube. You can always tell when you're the topic of conversation. For one thing, the conversation always cuts off when you appear suddenly. And if your appearance isn't sudden, if they can see you coming for several yards, at least one of them keeps looking in your direction so the chat can wrap up before you're actually in ear shot.

Aside from stretching at work, I wasn't sure what I had done to affront my cubicle neighbor. Surely a little yoga and herbal tea weren't clear signs of my witchy leanings.

I mean, I had also politely side-stepped a couple of church invitations when I first came to the job. Maybe that had put me on the wrong side of things. This area of the country is pretty conservative, but I didn't think people inside the 465 loop that surrounds Indianapolis were all that fanatical. Guardians of Faith Ministry notwithstanding.

So the Rules Lawyer didn't care for me, but I got on pretty well with a few other folks in the office. There were a selection of people I ate lunch with, when not doing yoga, and a couple of women that I walked around the building with on our company-enforced morning and afternoon breaks. I wouldn't call them close friends. I mean, I knew their names, but I never even called them by name in my own mind. It was Ginger Lunch Guy and Glasses Walking Girl. Very causal. Very uninvolved.

I didn't want to be too involved with my co-workers. I had my covenmates for actual friendship. Getting too buddy-buddy with co-workers could be a dangerous thing for someone like me. I'm not up for barbecues and beers at my place. In fact, the thought of one of these people in my home made me shiver. A wrong turn on the way to the bathroom would land them in our temple room. No, no, no, no. Bad, bad.

I was a good insurance claims adjuster, and I basically kept my nose down. My numbers were always on target. I was efficient. I was never involved in office drama. Just the sort of employee whom supervisors love.

My supervisor absolutely did not love me, though. He was indifferent to me, at best. It was unsettling. Based on my performance, he should have thought I was a rock star. At the very least, he should have been glad of my solid, efficient, consistent work. At my semi-annual performance reviews, though, he read off a list of my superlative skills like it was both tedious and cumbersome. I would normally have written this off to the boss hating his job, hating his life; but it seemed to be just me. He was engaged and gregarious every time the Rules Lawyer tapped on his door.

This is going to sound conceited, which is strange to me since I don't really value my looks all that highly. I mean, I'm a pretty woman (or so I'm told), but that's not how I see myself. And even if I did, it's not my greatest asset. Regardless of all that, I have noticed that most men react favorably to me. I attribute it to charm more than looks. I can be charming. I can make a person, male or female, feel like the center of the universe for a while. I make them the center of mine, and they get a little dizzy from the attention.

That's all it is, I think. People want the attention. They need it. We all need someone to laugh at our jokes, be interested in our stories, and enjoy our company. I've never considered it a superpower to be charming, although perhaps there is a hint of magic in the word. To *charm* someone is, by all rights, to cast a spell on them.

It was unsettling, then, for me to come against a man who was so unwaveringly immune to my charms. It's not like I was trying to swindle or trick him, either. I just wanted our interactions to be pleasant. But, try as I might, he doggedly avoided pleasantness in my presence.

I figured it could be worse. My boss wasn't quite a dick, and my cubicle neighbor was prissy to an annoying degree. These are first-world problems, as the saying goes.

Today's work was as monotonous and detail-ridden as any other. I pushed through the first couple of hours, getting most of my work done before the mid-morning break. I liked wrapping up early and covertly goofing off for the rest of the day. Sometimes I would work on my novel while pretending to review claims that I had already reviewed.

Just as I was getting ready to push away from my desk and lace up my walking shoes for the morning break and my daily walk, my cell phone vibrated in my purse. Lilly's face filled the screen. "Hey, lady. What's up?" I asked.

"You aren't going to believe what's happened," she said breathlessly. "Can you look at the Internet from your work computer?"

"Yeah," I shrugged, despite the fact that she couldn't see the gesture. "As long as I'm not looking at porn or shopping sites, they don't seem to care too much. I mean, I can't surf all day, but I can certainly peek."

I was already pulling up the browser as Lilly said, "Well, do a quick search for 'Indianapolis witch murder.'"

"Ye gods," I said. (I like the old swear words.) "Is that what we're calling it?"

"No, I think they're coming up with an even worse name. But this is easier to search for," she said. "You getting results?"

I scanned the top results from Google. A small picture of a woman in handcuffs accompanied the top story, which was titled

"Indianapolis Witch Arrested for Grisly Murder." The next two headlines were similar. I chose the *Washington Post's* write up.

"Is it someone we know?" I asked in a whisper.

"No, I don't think so," Lilly whispered in response. "At least, I don't know her. Maybe you do."

I read through the article. Sondra Little. Known witch. Height, weight, and hair color match the woman in the photograph. Confirmed member of Covenant of Solitaires, an international witchcraft ring.

I laughed out loud. One little bark of a laugh. "Witchcraft ring?" I whispered. "They're a bunch of isolated people trading cookie recipes on the Internet. They wouldn't know a spell from a sparkplug." I looked at Sondra's picture. She couldn't have been legal drinking age, and she looked terrified.

"That's exactly what I was thinking, too," Lilly said. "Plus, if she's a solitary witch, who were the two goons in the photograph with her?"

"Good point," I said. I looked away from the frightened woman's face in the photograph to look back at the article. "Looks like they are going to be questioning her about her accomplices. Jesus Christ, this sounds just like the medieval witch hunts all over again. You don't think they'll torture the poor kid, do you?"

Lilly snorted. "You mean, 'enhanced interrogation techniques?' I honestly wouldn't put it past them. If Homeland Security takes over this case, as rumors are starting to suggest they might, then I would almost count on it. Those Guardians of Faith people are now spouting off about magical terrorism."

Silence for a moment. My mind spun through all the implications. This was a nightmare. My heart hurt for the girl that I knew had to be innocent. A solitary is a witch alone, usually a witch without training. A witch with very little mojo to tap. Sure, the odd solitary had come from a coven and been trained. Yes, the very rare solitary had great power and skill. I suppose a few solitaries could come together to pull off a potent bit of magic, if they were motivated.

47

The truth is that most solitary witches are very happy to work alone. They learn what they need from the spirits and from nature directly, and they thumb their noses at cloistered and secretive coven types like me and my friends.

A harder truth is that only a very experienced witch with training, resources, and an axe to grind would have done the sort of magic we saw evidenced in the photographs of the murder. This young woman couldn't be old enough to have undergone the training that would have allowed her to commit this ritual murder.

"It isn't her," I said. "They have the wrong person."

"I know," Lilly replied. "I know."

"We have to do something," I said.

"Any ideas?"

"I have a couple of ideas," I admitted. "But let's get everyone together after work tonight to see what they think."

"I'll muster the troops," she said. "We'll see you tonight."

The call disconnected, and I pocketed my phone, one hand still operating the mouse on my computer. An idea had flashed in my head. That symbol from the murderess's robes. I knew I had seen it before. The Covenant of Solitaires web page finally loaded, and there was the symbol. Of course! The real culprit must have been trying to point the finger at someone in CoS. Was she aiming at sweet little Sondra on purpose, or was the girl an easy blond target?

I closed the browser to take a pee break before coming back to my desk for the last of the actual work I needed to accomplish today. I anticipated that I would be jotting notes about how my coven could intervene on behalf of Sondra without getting swept up in the tempest that was starting to rage in our city.

My plans were shot to hell when I returned to my cubicle, though. The Rules Lawyer was standing next to our boss, waiting for me to return. She had a look of triumph on her face, which worried me. She was making eye contact for the first time in months. I think that worried me more.

"Ms. Wheeler," he said. Wait. Now *he* wasn't looking me in the eye. "I need to speak with you in my office, please."

"Certainly," I said. Rules Lawyer gave me a very smug grin and then disappeared behind the wall of her cube.

Boss Man closed the door behind me, and indicated the chair I should sit in.

"It has come to my attention that you have not been using your work time in an appropriate manner." He paused. I think he was waiting for me to confirm or deny his statement. I wasn't sure what he was talking about, so I said nothing at all. He continued, "We have records showing that you have sat at your computer for long periods of time without significantly modifying the documents on your screen. We also have records showing your personal use of the Internet during work hours." Another pause from him. More silence from me. "Do you have anything to say about this?"

I steadied myself with a deep breath. I could feel the heat in my cheeks, and I knew my blood pressure had just skyrocketed. I imagined that my face and chest were covered in red splotches that vied for intensity with my hair. Anger was really not a good look on me. I blame the Irish and Dutch ancestry.

"All I can say is that I have been a good worker, Mr. Reynolds," I began. "I have taken some down time, perhaps, but only after completing all the work I could reasonably do in a day. I very rarely use the Internet for anything not related to a claim."

He met my eyes as he asked, "And how is Covenant of Solitaires related to any auto claim?"

I dropped my head and bit my lips together. Arguing wasn't going to help. I couldn't take the high road here. I had absolutely looked at a witchcraft site at work. The best I could do is hope I hadn't found my way into more trouble than a reprimand. Even getting fired would be better than what was happening to Sondra.

"It isn't related," I admitted. "I was merely curious about the news surrounding this whole mess. It has the whole city talking."

"The whole country is talking, Ms. Wheeler," he said. "But you are to look into these great social and political matters on your own time."

Okay, Rose. Take your lumps so you can get back to work. Don't let your pride get you angry enough to say or do something rash.

"This company takes these issues very seriously, Ms. Wheeler."

Here comes the big smack on the hands with a ruler.

"I'm afraid we're letting you go."

Wait. What?

"Pardon me?" I asked. I'm certain I looked dumbfounded. I felt like I'd missed part of the conversation somewhere. Who gets fired for doing all their work in a timely way and being on the Internet for a minute and a half?

"I need you to gather the things from your desk and report to human resources," Boss Man said. "A security guard is waiting at your desk with a box for your personal things. You are not permitted to take any files or manuals with you. He will then escort you to HR, where you will complete an exit interview and turn in your key badge before leaving the premises. Thank you, and good day."

I was so stunned by the dismissiveness in my dismissal that I reacted in silent slow-motion. I walked the few feet back to my desk where the security guard was keeping watch over my training manuals and claims files. There was a piece of paper on my chair. Printed in capital letters was a single, blocky word. "WITCH."

I looked around at the people in the nearby cubes. A couple were talking to each other and looking nervously my way. Most had their backs to me, theoretically immersed in their work. Rules Lawyer was conspicuously absent. I crumpled the paper and tossed it into her cube.

What did I even have here that was worth keeping? A Shakespeare bobblehead, a potted plant, a few of those twisty metal puzzles where the object was to separate the pieces. I didn't have any pictures on my desk. No art from a toddler to proudly display. Just junk.

I packed up my junk and left.

Chapter 7

I tossed the pathetic box of junk from my cubicle onto the floor by the sofa. I would sort it out later. Only my Shakespeare bobblehead and pothos ivy were rescued from the box and placed in proper position on a bookshelf. The rest could wait.

I put the kettle on the stove for my evening tea. Lavender, chamomile, and lemon balm. If that wouldn't soothe my jangled nerves, I'd make something stronger after the coven left. Valerian and skullcap would relax me right to sleep. They would also make the house smell like sweaty gym socks.

My bra came off as I walked toward my bedroom. One thing I was going to love about unemployment – no bra.

Unemployment. Shit, I would need to drive out to the unemployment office in Plainfield to file. I had never done that before. Then again, I had never been fired or laid off. Hurray for firsts.

I said a little prayer of thanks for the house being paid off. I hadn't managed that on my meager salary, of course. My parents had bought the house for me when they sold a large piece of Iowa farmland to a biofuel company. My name was on the title, along with theirs, so that when they died I wouldn't be fined estate taxes for inheriting the house. My lack of mortgage was a blessing right now.

I pulled out the notebook where I kept a running to-do list. I added *file for unemployment* and *research freelance writing* to the list. I felt confident that Grace and I would be able to keep the lights and water running and ourselves fed.

I pulled out a brown case folder from my desk. Inside was not a case, but a novel I had begun writing earlier this year, the outline and character notes clipped to the top left brackets with the story itself clipped into the right side prongs. I'd only ever poked around at writing, but I knew I had talent. My pseudonymous articles had appeared in popular witchcraft magazines, where practically everyone published under a pen name.

I skimmed my outline, pleased that I still found my story compelling. I clicked my laptop to life and placed the folder next to it like an open-faced literary sandwich. The kettle whistled for me from the kitchen, and I heeded its call.

No sooner had I reached the stove than Pearl and her daughter Beatrice came tumbling through the door. Pearl's face was livid, and Bea's was tear-streaked and swollen. Pearl threw her bags and jackets in a heap near my junk box and then rummaged through one of the totes for Bea's dolls and coloring books.

"Stay in here while Mommy talks to Aunt Rose, okay?" Pearl told the child.

"What's going on?" I asked. I knew I was about to hear exactly what was happening in great detail, but it's always best to engage directly.

"I don't even know where to start," Pearl said. Her voice had raised by half an octave, which told me just how angry she was. She gets a bit shrieky when she's about to go ballistic.

I got out two more cups and tea-balls. Pearl and Bea needed a nerve tonic, too, from the sounds of it. I'd add several ice cubes to child's.

"Did something happen at Bea's school?" I asked.

"Oh, boy, did something happen," Pearl huffed and shook her head. "My darling daughter doesn't know to keep some things a secret, no matter how many times I tell her. I think she learned today, the hard way." She took a sip of the hot tea. "She knows we're witches, of course."

I nodded. Bea was only seven, but there were certain magics that she had been shown. Her choice to become a witch herself was still years away, but she was old enough to understand the basic principles of her mother's religion. After all, children of other faiths are taught their parents' beliefs while they are still in the cradle. We, at least, waited until a child had reached the age of reason. Our aim was not to indoctrinate a minor who was too young to consent to our practices and beliefs. Rather, we sought to provide an option for our children, should they choose to follow us in the old ways.

"Well, she decided to tell the kids in her class," Pearl added in exasperation. "With everything that's going on, they freaked out. The teacher said they were shouting at her and throwing rocks." Pearl was practically shouting now, and I couldn't say I blamed her.

"What did the teacher do?" I asked. "Is Beatrice okay?"

"The teacher pulled Bea off the playground and took her to the principal's office. The principal called me to come get her. When I get there, the principal tells me the whole story and then waits to see if I'm going to agree that yes we are witches. She tried to ask me three different ways without coming out and asking me."

"What did you tell her?" I asked.

Pearl raised an eyebrow and affected her best offended voice. "I told her that I am an accountant, a regular wizard with numbers, and the last time I checked that didn't need to get put on some stupid magical index."

I nodded my approval. "And how is Bea?" I took the little girl her iced tea in a plastic cup I kept around just for her. It was yellow with daisies and honeybees on its surface.

Pearl's face turned to a pained expression as her attention shifted from the bullies at school to her beloved daughter. She stroked Bea's hair, which was a few shades lighter than Pearl's. "I think she's going to be okay. She has some bruises and a couple of scrapes. I think her heart hurts more than her body."

Pearl's cell phone rang from within the recesses of the many bags she had brought. "Shit. It's John." She marched down the hall, her shoulders squared for another confrontation with her ex-husband, Bea's father.

I'd never actually met the man, but to hear Pearl tell it, he is a fiend in bed – and out of it. The sex had always been great, but he was both stubborn and mean. The couple had divorced when Bea was still a baby, and now John had a new family and a growing interest in seeing his daughter. The trouble was that Bea always came home crying after a trip to her dad's house, and she would act up in school for a day or two after her return.

"WHAT?" I heard Pearl explode from the hallway. "That is the most ludicrous thing I have ever heard!" Bea cringed each time her mother shouted. "Oh, you did, huh? Well, we'll see about that. If you want to fight this battle with me, buddy, let's go. I'll see you in court."

"What was all that about?" I asked.

Pearl's face and neck were covered in red splotches. She was gritting her teeth as she responded. "THAT was my asshole ex. He says he got a call from the principal, as well. He went in to talk with the bitch, and he says that he now has all the proof he needs to take Bea away from me forever."

"That doesn't make sense," I said. I could feel my eyebrows touching as they came together in irritated disbelief. "The accusations of children on a playground aren't any sort of evidence at all."

"Right, but he says Bea has said some things to him while she was visiting," Pearl replied. Bea dropped her head and started crying. Pearl picked her up. "Baby, I'm not mad at you. I'm mad at your father." She held the little girl close to her chest and rocked her. "Daddy doesn't understand about what Mommy does. That's why it needs to be a secret."

I didn't love that a second-grader needed to be taught secrecy. It felt icky somehow. Still, you either teach the child to keep silent or you don't teach them anything about the Craft. It is said within the Craft that the ancient Sphinx conveys four magical powers to the seeker – knowledge, will, courage, and silence. To grow as a witch, you must study, you must act, you must master your fears, and you must keep silent about much of what you have learned and done. Ours is an art that is practiced in the shadows. The average person fears and despises the power that we have gained through study and self-mastery.

Pearl continued talking over Bea's head while they rocked. "He said he hired a private investigator a few months ago. He supposedly has pictures of us performing a ritual around a bonfire in the woods."

I almost snorted tea out of my nose. "You mean the cookout we had for Labor Day? That was harmless. It was a campfire, some John Mellencamp tunes, and a weenie roast."

Pearl nodded. "I know. But he says the pictures tell a different story. He says we are dancing and chanting around a witch fire, summoning the Devil, and branding Bea."

I couldn't even respond to that. Well, okay, we had summoned Robin, but not on that night, and certainly not with Bea present. My own blood was rising in my chest and face at the idea that we had hurt Pearl's child, or any child. The idea was antithetical to everything we held sacred. I was finally able to stammer, "Why would he think that we branded her?"

Pearl shook her head. "Do you recall that she got burned a little? A spark from the bonfire, a little firefly, landed on her chest. I used your burn salve, and she was fine. But it left a mark for a few days. He took pictures of it. He says it looks like a symbol, a witch mark. He says the pictures show one of us holding a branding iron."

"That's just not possible," I said. "None of us ..." I stopped short and dropped my head. Looking back up at Pearl, I said, "The roasting fork? The thing we put the hotdogs on. Maybe that's what is in the picture?"

She nodded. "Maybe so. That's the only thing it could be."

We sat in silence for a moment. The audacity of the situation flowed around us. Surely a good lawyer would be able to help Pearl get this nonsense set to rights. But could she afford a good lawyer? She might only be able to afford a mediocre one. John could certainly afford a good lawyer. In fact, he might be able to tie her up in court costs and lawyer fees long enough to steal Bea away. Worse yet, Pearl would serve jail time if it was proven that she intentionally scarred her child. And with the fervor surrounding the witchcraft murder, her situation could easily shift from absurd to desperate.

"Where is Robin?" Pearl asked after we had stewed in silence, each of us sipping her tea. "I thought he would be here with you?"

"He and Grace went to pick up some of the supplies we need for our protection spell," I said. Grace only worked at the New Age shop three days a week, so she had time to relax and take care of a few errands. "I called Grace after Lilly called me at work today." My thoughts turned bitter for a moment. "I can't prove it, but I think that snotty bint in the cube next to me overheard my conversation, jumped to an accurate conclusion, and ran to the boss to accuse me."

"That sucks, Rose," Pearl consoled. "What are you going to do?"

"Live off the God-fearing taxpayers of Indiana for as long as I can and write smutty stories about witches," I said with a wink.

Pearl toasted me with her teacup. "Perfect."

We finished our tea, and Bea climbed back out of her mom's lap to play in the floor again. She chattered to her doll as she arranged its living environment with a tissue box, her mother's bags, and a blanket. The doll walked and prattled around its little world, while Pearl and I cleared away the cups and kettle and sat in comfortable silence waiting for our friends to arrive.

Lilly came through the door first, followed closely by Evaline. We hugged our hellos. I offered them tea, laughing to myself that I was practically British with my ubiquitous beverage choice. They declined and refilled their own water bottles before settling in.

Lilly unpacked several small amber, brown, and green bottles from her coven bag. "I brought some things that we might want for our spell tonight," she said. "I mixed them all myself. "Florida water, fiery wall of protection oil, black cat oil, and seven holy waters."

"Wow," I said. That was an impressive list of potions to bring for this spell. "When did you start making these?"

"I like to keep some of them around all the time," Lilly shared. "But I began replenishing my supply when Sewall first came up with that blasted index. I was worried then that we would need to protect ourselves."

"You have no idea," Pearl said, and then she launched into her recounting of Bea's attack at school and her ex-husband's asinine accusations. Robin and Grace came home half way through the retelling, and she backtracked to tell it from the beginning. When she finished, they all looked at her through masks of shock and anger.

"You were right to gather the coven, Rose," Robin said. "This is a turbulent time, and vengeful forces are already at work in this city. You all need protection, and I hope I am able to lend power to your rite this evening."

We all nodded. It was that slow nod of the determined but daunted. I patted Robin's hand. "You've had several days of rest, love. I'm sure you'll be able to lend a marginal amount of power, at the very least."

"Marginal isn't why you summoned me," he said with a shrug.

"Well, I'm not worried about it," I said. "I imagine that we will have other battles to fight, other spells to perform, other rites to enact before all is said and done with Sewall and his followers. You have plenty of time left in this conflict to be the big hero."

Darkness was still an hour or so away, and we wanted the cover of darkness to work our spell. There's a reason witches wear black robes and do their magic under dark skies. You can be invisible without having to work up the energy for a glamouring, a spell that changes other people's perception of you. We were taught to wear black and work with the shadows so that our vital life force could be directed more efficiently toward our intended targets.

Lilly measured and cut long strands of Evaline's homespun yarn for each of us. Pearl separated and wound the threads into neat bundles so they wouldn't tangle while we worked. Grace gathered bone beads, while I prepared the swallow tail-feathers she and Robin had purchased from a local magical supplier. Evaline bustled around the kitchen, gathering the bowls and plates that we always seemed to need in our magical workings. In the midst of all these other preparations, Robin sat in the floor with Bea and colored a picture of a pony.

When the time had finally arrived to don our robes and slide under the night sky, all our supplies were gathered into baskets and bowls for easy portage. Bea rubbed her eyes and twisted her loose robe around her body like it was a potato sack. I put my finger to my lips as a reminder that we were going to be very quiet until we were in our special place.

The coven slipped through the back door onto the unlit deck and out into the dark woods. We didn't dare light a candle, since our unfenced garden was visible from both of our neighbors' houses. Luckily, we knew a nifty bit of magic that would spare our eyes the strain of working without a light in the moonless woods.

We went deep into the trees until we came to a small clearing with a fire ring at its center. We had used this place several times for spells and Sabbats. Like the house, it was warded with energetic protections that kept our mundane neighbors at bay. Grace and I had gone so far as to establish a useful fiction in their minds. We had allowed ourselves to be seen, once or twice each year, drinking hard ciders while relaxing around a baby campfire. Just two country girls enjoying the quiet life. Nothing to see here. Move along.

Tonight, our need-fire would be lit, but it would be completely unseen by the muggles. Lilly arranged the sacred woods which included birch, holly, oak, pine, hazel, elm, rowan, willow, and yew. "Nine woods in the cauldron go. Burn them fast and burn them slow," she chanted softly as she plied the string of the coven's oak bow around the ash stick. Those survivalist shows could learn something from witches. We all knew how to start a fire without matches or lighter fluid, even though we only tested the skill a few times in our lives. A need-fire wasn't used for everyday protection spells. It was only lit when great danger threatened a coven or the village they tended.

While Lilly lit the fire, Grace and I walked the boundaries of our circle, each moving in the opposite direction and marking the circle on the ground with our staves. Neither of us spoke, but as we crossed paths and returned to our starting point, the noises of the forest became muffled and indistinct. The witches' compass was laid out around us, Grace and I taking our places at the northern and southern points of the circle. Evaline stood at the easternmost edge, and Pearl held Bea by her side at the westernmost point. Lilly stood near the small fire she had built, her hands outstretched toward it, energy flowing into the flames. I knew with unwavering faith that those flames were invisible to anyone who might venture past our hallowed spot in the woods.

Robin walked a wide circle around the little fire. "This is good work, my dears," he said. "Pass over the fire to feel its purification, its guardianship of your lives and homes." He leaped over the flames, grinning as he went. I hitched the skirts of my robes up over my knees and made a running jump over the fire. Evaline was next, as lithe and nimble as a deer. Lilly took one fast but firm step over the flame. Grace, fretting a little just before she ran, made a clumsy but effective jump.

Pearl hesitated. "I'm afraid to do it with Bea in my arms, and she's too small to do it herself."

Robin lifted the child away from her mother's side and held her close as he passed over the flame once more. Bea giggled and snuggled her face into his chest. Pearl made her jump and then took Beatrice back to their position.

I passed the basket of yarn over the flames. "We call on the Witch Mother to protect her children this night and for all the nights to come." I passed the basket of beads and feathers over the fire. "We call on the power of the Witch Father to protect his daughters as we face a great enemy."

Each of us chose bundles of yarn, strung beads on the threads, and spoke the first words of our incantation. "By knot of one, this spell's begun." We braided the strands together with the swallow tail feathers. We were intent on our work, each of us rocking, seething, as we braided. Robin continued walking around us as we worked, humming a tune that was at once familiar and foreign, like something I'd heard in a dream or another lifetime. My braid was the only thing I could see, and my fingers worked swiftly. I was finished first, which was no surprise, and I started helping little Bea who was playing with the beads and feathers that were left in the basket.

"Pick at least three beads," I told her, "and at least one feather." She chose seven beads and four feathers. Alright. Her braided ladder would have lots of rungs. "Now, tell the feathers, the beads, and the yarn that you want them to keep bad people, bad words, and bad accidents far from you." She held her components in her hands and whispered what I had said. "It's time to braid them," I said. "Do you know what this charm is called?"

"A braid," she said.

"It is a braid," I agreed. "But we call it a ladder."

She scrunched up her nose in disbelief. "You can't climb on this at all."

I chuckled. "I know. But you can use this sort of ladder in lots of ways, as you'll learn. And some of them do help you climb high into the world of thoughts and visions."

She didn't believe me.

"Okay," I settled. "Maybe it's a silly name. But the magic works."

This, she seemed fine with. I showed her how to braid the strands together, sliding a bead into place here, adding a feather there. Her clumsy fingers gave it a try for a few plaits before handing it back to me. Good. She worked some of the magic herself. That would help. The others were finishing their braids, and they passed Bea's ladder amongst them, each taking a turn at offering the coven's only child their own protective energy.

We tied the remaining knots as a group, chanting the remainder of the spell together.

"By knot of two, our guard is true." The second knot was tied into the end of each of our braids.

"By knot of three, no harm to me." The third knot was tied into the middle of the cord.

We would tie the fourth and fifth knots into the spaces between the middle knot and each of the ends. "By knot of four, this power I store. By knot of five, this power contrive."

I could see a glow and feel a thrum of magic around the braided and knotted cord. Our work wasn't at an end, though.

"By knot of six, this spell I fix. By knot of seven, protection's given."

My cord felt hot in my hands. Electric. "By knot of eight, I seal this fate."

I formed the final knot in the cord between my fingers, and I saw in my mind the wall of fire surrounding myself and my coven. I knew as I pulled the ninth and final knot tight that our spell would deflect the greatest blows of the upcoming fight from us. "By knot of nine, protection's mine."

"So mote it be," whispered Pearl.

"So mote it be," said Lilly.

"By the power of three times three, as we do will, so mote it be," intoned Robin.

Chapter 8

I was a latch key kid of divorced parents, and an only child at that, which meant that I had a good amount of alone time growing up. That rarely happens for me as an adult. Grace didn't work on the weekends, and we often had the coven or other houseguests staying overnight or longer. I loved our nomadic herd of friends – the belly dancer and yoga teacher who wintered with us, the mask-maker who couch surfed between Renaissance fairs and Pagan festivals, the Army vet who needed a place to sink his roots back into American soil after years in Germany. Our most recent houseguest defied description. "Newly manifested witchcraft elder spirit?" There was always somebody coming or going, and we loved it that way.

Today, though, I reveled in the solitude of an empty house. It was me, my house rabbit, and Grace's black cat. The bunny, whom I had named Anyanka as a tribute to a rabbit-phobic demon on *Buffy the Vampire Slayer*, was roaming freely as I puttered around the house. She was a sable Rex, my very own velveteen rabbit.

I sipped my morning tea, a mild and tasty tonic featuring nettles, dandelion root, and peppermint while watching Anyanka run and kick on our sun porch. I'd kept rabbits since I was a young teen, always as pets. For whatever reason, I was never able to eat rabbit meat without getting ill. Whether it was a psychological aversion or a physical allergy didn't matter to me. Rabbit was not on my menu.

You'd be surprised how many men like to jokingly threaten to eat your pet when said pet is a rabbit. Women never do this, not to me. But nearly every man who had occasion to know I kept a rabbit as a pet made some reference to hasenpfeffer or rabbit stew. By the time Grace's dad made the lame and ubiquitous joke, I'd had enough. "You can eat my rabbit, Dan," I'd said, leaning in across the table and smiling, "right after I eat your dog." Houdini, the aging Lhasa Apso, whimpered under my chair.

Anya did a helicopter jump and then bolted in the direction of the cat, who ran. Anya was bigger than the cat in question, whose name was Rue. Anya chased Rue to the far side of the sun room where the cat was forced to turn and face down her pursuer. Putting a protective paw in the air, ready to strike if need be, Rue held her ground until the rabbit turned and sprinted away. This time the cat chased the rabbit until they reached a wall. Turn, again.

More chasing. Back and forth, the game of tag continued until both girls sprawled on the floor facing each other in happy exhaustion.

Grace was at work today, and Robin had gone to stay with Pearl and Bea for a few days. He and I agreed that Pearl and her daughter needed some special attention, some extra protection.

I fetched my laptop from my bedroom and returned to the sunroom to work on my novel. I had been struck with inspiration after our ritual last night, and I wanted to write while the words seemed to flow freely.

The story wasn't going to become a classic, an icon of great literature. It was a paranormal romance wrapped in a cozy mystery package. A smutty, supernatural, whodunit. The main character, of course, resembled me in many ways, and the cast of characters who played backup to my heroine looked and sounded a lot like my best friends. Details were shifted to line up more poetically, and the magic was completely unrealistic. "Who would want to read a paranormal book with real magic in it?" I asked the room. Anyanka didn't know, either. "It looks pretty boring from the outside, most of the time." Real magic, the kind my coven does, the kind all witches in the real world do, just doesn't look like much of anything to an observer.

I mean, okay, the bit of manifestation we did with Robin would have looked pretty cool. But most magic happens on the subtle planes, those inner and outer realms that are unseen. It is real and potent, but there isn't a great deal of showmanship. No smoke, no mirrors, no inanimate objects moving at the will of the witch. At least, not usually.

My novel, I determined, needed to have more of the Hollywood magic that readers expected. And sex. Lots and lots of steamy sex.

Robin, it turns out, was a muse for me. Thinking about his eyes, his scent, his arms wrapped around me in lust or lifted to the heavens in power brought scenes and plot devices into my mind and through my hands. I sat in the sunroom typing until the battery died on my laptop and my bunny had long since hopped away to her den in my bedroom.

When I finally looked up from my work, I felt satisfied but shaky. The light had shifted outside my windows, and I suddenly realized that hours had passed without food or water. I was running on the morning's tea, and it was now pushing into the early evening. Grace wouldn't be home until 9 pm or so, and I normally had dinner ready when she arrived. I couldn't wait that long to eat, though.

I headed to the kitchen to figure out short-term food, when my phone rang. Pearl.

"Hey, hon. How are things going with Robin?" I asked.

"Oh my goat," she replied breathlessly. I could hear the giggle in her tone. "Whew! That man is … wow. I don't have words."

"Oh?" I asked. A hot flush creeped through my neck, a prickly jealousy that was mixed with curiosity and excitement. Had they had sex? Seriously? I tried to sound unaffected. "What's going on?"

More giggling. "I'll tell you all about it when you get here."

I paused a moment. "Am I coming over?"

Giggle. "Sorry. My brain isn't working quite right," she said. And then, pulling herself together, "I'm trying to get you and Lilly to come help me with a healing for Bea. All her poor bruises look terrible today. I thought the three of us plus Robin could take care of it together."

Evaline must be at work today, too.

"Sure, honey. I can come over," I said. "What time?"

"As soon as you're able. I'm ordering pizza for us. Any preferences?" she asked.

"Oh, you know me," I laughed. "Get whatever you like. I'll pick off the snausages."

"Okay," she bubbled. "See you soon."

I didn't usually love that the drive to Pearl's house took an hour. It was one of the drawbacks to living in the country. Today, I appreciated the time to gather my thoughts and explore how I felt about the possibility of Robin and Pearl being intimate.

I consider myself a polyamorous person. That means that I know I am capable of loving and being intimate with more than one person at a time. The truth is, though, I've not really had much experience in poly relationships. Grace and I were sometimes lovers, more often friends, and we had both had relationships outside of what we shared with each other. I had never had a pang of jealousy where she was concerned. What was different here?

For one thing, I'd not had a close friend get intimate with someone I considered a lover. And Robin was a new lover for me. Very new. That was strange considering that he and I had been spiritual consorts for years. Was it the longevity of our spiritual relationship or the newness of our physical one that was bringing up my own possessiveness? I couldn't tell.

I took several deep breaths to lower my blood pressure. I could feel the pulse of blood behind my eyes. I was almost seeing red, quite literally, and I knew my reaction wasn't fair to me, to Robin, or to Pearl. After all, she had been having her own relationship with Robin for years, too. We all had. Why had I assumed that the sex he shared with me was only reserved for me? I hadn't even realized I'd made that assumption until it was challenged.

Of course, I could also be jumping to conclusions. Maybe Pearl wasn't giddy from sex with Robin at all. Maybe sex is just how I relate to him, so I assume she would do the same.

No. There was sex. I shouldn't convince myself otherwise. Denial would only prolong my need to deal with my feelings about it. That wouldn't help in the long run. In fact, it would probably make it worse.

I took some more deep breaths. I couldn't hear my heartbeat pounding in my ears anymore. That was an improvement.

By the time I pulled into Pearl's apartment complex, I felt calm. If I was honest with myself, I would have even admitted that

I felt excited about hearing Pearl's story. Robin was an incredible lover. Why wouldn't I want that for my friend?

I shook my head to clear it of the confusing and ultimately weird questions that were rolling through my brain. The shake didn't clear them away, but it gave me a moment to refocus and knock on the door.

It was Robin who met me. He stepped into the hallway, the door at his back nearly closed.

"Hello, my love," he said in that wonderful accent just before leaning in for a kiss that curled my toes and hardened my nipples.

I blushed as he pulled away. "Hello," I said. Where were we? What had I been worried about a moment ago? I couldn't remember.

"I've missed you," he confided, "though I've enjoyed getting to know Pearl."

Oh, yeah. I remembered.

"What is this frown?" he asked.

"Nothing," I said. "I'm just ...." Damn it. What was I? What feeling was this? "I'm just feeling insecure, I guess."

He tilted my chin back up so that I was looking into those light-filled amber eyes again. "Never doubt your place in my heart," he said. "I have loved you beyond time, beyond space. You are my Rose."

Something in my heart eased. I relaxed into his embrace, and I found myself surprised by the emotions that welled up in me where Robin was concerned. How could I feel so fiercely about him in such a short time? Yes, the spiritual affair had to be accounted, but still. This was all so new and strange. This man felt like my husband. My mate. Mine.

Maybe not only mine, though. I had no claim on him. He wasn't property, after all. I forced myself to loosen my grip on him, both physically and metaphorically. I felt a tightness ease in my chest. If he were *mine*, that didn't mean he was only mine.

Could I be okay with Pearl claiming whatever piece of Robin that he offered to her? Another deep breath, more space in my heart. Yes, I probably could. I loved Pearl, and I wanted happiness for her. If having some sort of relationship with Robin made her happy, then I was okay with that. Probably.

I had to suspend this line of thought for myself, at least for the next few hours. It was going to do nothing but make me cranky if I had to keep chasing my own tail on this topic. Nothing was going to get decided right this minute, even in my own mind. And I still hadn't witnessed Robin and Pearl together or heard about their escapades. I might be brewing a tempest in an herbal teapot. For the tenth time since receiving Pearl's phone call, I instructed myself to breathe and relax.

Robin gave my shoulder a squeeze as we entered the apartment. His hand lingered at the small of my back, and I relished the light contact with him.

Pearl came sweeping across the room to hug me. "There's the prettiest Rose in the garden," she said, enfolding me in an effervescent embrace. "I'm so glad you could come help us."

She was glowing. Seriously. A light was pouring through her, and she seemed so alive and happy. I couldn't help but feel happy for her.

"Lilly will be here soon," she said. "We'll get started after she gets here. For now, let's just talk."

I plopped down on her sofa, ditching my shoes and pulling my feet under me where I sat. "I'm wishing we had done something bigger than the protection ladders last night. Lilly and I had been talking about something more all-encompassing just before I got fired. Evaline was going to pick up some things, and then we just spaced it, between mine and Bea's bad day."

"Yeah, matters close to home sort of took over," Pearl agreed. "I guess it always comes down to that. We gotta look out for our family before anyone else."

I nodded. These women were my family, and I would do anything to keep them safe.

"We need to figure out two things," I said. "First, how big a threat are the Guardians of Faith, really? And second, who is truly behind the murder of that man?"

"And third," Pearl added, "when will Robin be ready to kick in some serious mojo to our efforts?"

"That's an excellent question," I said, looking at the man himself. "How are you feeling?"

"Stronger every day," he said, flexing his dusky bicep and winking.

"Has Miss Pearl been taking care of you?" I almost didn't want to know the answer.

"She's a good girl, a good hostess, and a good healer," Robin said, kissing Pearl on the forehead. She beamed like she had gotten a gold star.

"Speaking of good girls," Pearl said, "I had better go check on Bea. You wanna come with me, Rose?" Her eyebrows arched dramatically and she was nodding toward the back of the apartment with the top of her head. Nope, there was no way Robin would suspect she wanted alone time with me to gossip about him. Pearl was obviously very subtle.

Robin winked as I followed Pearl. He mumbled something about letting Lilly in and taking care of the pizza.

Pearl gave Bea a very cursory check before pulling me into her bedroom. She sprawled on her bed and fanned herself as if she was having a hot flash right now.

"Ohmygod, he's so amazing," she gushed.

"Yeah," I said.

"It's weird, though," she said. "I mean, we had sex, and it was incredible, but that isn't even what makes me think he is so amazing."

"Oh?" I asked. My curiosity was at war with my jealousy. I wasn't sure how much detail I wanted. I probably wouldn't know my limit until I'd passed it, in fact.

"Yeah," she continued. "I mean, when I look at him or even just hear him speak, I think how sexy he is. But when I have the chance to be near him, I just want to snuggle."

I must have looked skeptical. I felt skeptical. Pearl looked at my disbelieving expression and shrugged. "Like I said, the sex was awesome, but it was the way he held me and talked to me afterward that was the best part. He makes me feel calm, like everything's going to be okay."

"That's great, honey," I said. "I'm glad he gives you that." I was, too.

"Did you guys do it when he was at your house?" she asked. "Did Grace?

I blushed, and I think my face was as red as my hair. Pearl laughed conspiratorially. "I knew it!" she exclaimed. "Well, he had sex with all of us in fantasies and dreams before we conjured him, right? I figured it only makes sense that it would happen in the flesh, too."

"Maybe, yeah," I said. "He and I did. But he and Grace haven't yet. At least I don't think so. They haven't really been alone together yet."

"He hasn't had any time with Lilly and Evaline yet, either," Pearl said. "But I do think it'll happen. Even if it's only just once with each of us."

I squirmed where I sat. "How does that make you feel?" I asked. "Are you okay fucking a guy that every single one of your coven sisters has been with? Doesn't it seem kind of ... I don't know ... trashy?"

Pearl look at me like I was crazy. Or stupid. She laughed, saying, "We conjured this devil up with a sex ritual. He may not be the actual Devil that Christians are always worrying about, not Satan. But he is all about lust and magic and mystery and the dark woods. Of course there's going to be sex. And lots of it, I imagine."

She had a point. I needed to let go of my inner prude. I should have guessed from the beginning that the sex would continue beyond the conjuring. It was the fuel that brought him here, and it was probably the fodder that would keep him with us in this physical plane.

We went back to the public rooms of the apartment just as Lilly arrived. Pizza followed hot on her heels, and we all ate and talked and laughed before turning our attentions to the healing we had come to do.

When we did focus on the work at hand, Pearl made her daughter a soft bed on the floor while Lilly and I lit candles. We untied our long hair and sang while Robin drew the witch's compass around us all.

Pearl knelt in the center and called on the healing powers of the four gates. Wind of breath, stone of bone, water of blood, and fire that is the life force within us all. She pulled the vital energies into her body, as did Lilly, Robin, and I. Into our bodies and then around the circle, sharing our energy and the energies of the elements until it was flowing out of our hands. We then each laid our hands onto Bea. Pearl ran her hands over the child's arms and legs, aiming her potent healing power at the bruises and pains of her physical body. My hands stayed at her heart, focusing on restoring her faith, hope, and love. Lilly worked healing magic for the little girl's mind, helping to clear away the worry and fear that was trying to take root. Robin's hands cupped the soles of Bea's feet, circulating all of the energy through the child evenly and making sure no part was missed.

Like I always say, magic doesn't usually look very impressive to a casual observer. We were four adults kneeling around a child and praying. The impressive part of magic is rarely the pyrotechnics and flash of movie wizardry. What impresses real witches is that when Bea sat up, she was calm, smiling, and bore no trace of the marks with which she had laid down.

Chapter 9

We wanted to see what we were up against in regards to the fanatical minister and his church of zealots. We needed to see for ourselves and not through the lens of the local media. To that end, we decided to do some reconnaissance behind enemy lines. That's a clandestine way of saying that our coven decided to go to church.

Grace was a hold out. She thought it was a foolish plan that would only draw attention to the members of the coven. She had another panic attack, and Robin held and soothed her back to a place of calm before tucking her in bed for the night. She had worn herself out with fear, not unlike the dormouse from *Alice and Wonderland.* Apparently, Robin had the jam to dot on her nose so she could get tucked away into her teapot.

The rest of us felt sure about going to witness the Guardians of Faith in person. We all felt like we could blend in well enough not to draw undue attention. Besides, it's not like witches are green hags in pointy hats. Nor do we get struck by lightning trying to enter a church. Without our pentacles and ritual robes, we looked like an accountant, a hipster, a reformed Goth, and a boho-hippie.

Lilly and I agreed to tone down our looks a bit, just in case. Robin posed as Pearl's husband, holding Bea's hand. I brought my Bible and distributed extras to my covenmates. One benefit of growing up Baptist: I had lots of Bibles. Mine even sported silver engraved letters spelling my name – a graduation gift from my former pastor.

None of my coven sisters had grown up with the same sort of fundamentalist Christianity as me. I had gone to Baptist school all through elementary, and I'd had to attend church Sunday morning, Sunday night, and Wednesday night through high school. That was to say nothing of getting visited by church elders on Thursday evenings and going to youth group on Fridays and Saturdays.

It wasn't like the girls had never been inside a church, of course. It was just different. Pearl had been raised within the Spiritualist church, and Evelyn had attended a few services at friends' churches. Lilly and Grace had been raised almost devoid of religion, only going to churches for weddings and funerals, and finding the whole thing showy and strange.

Conservative, fundamentalist, evangelical churches, in my opinion, are a strange mixture of warm welcomes and outright loathing. From the moment you walk through the doors, right up until the moment the actual preaching begins, your shoulders are hugged, your hand is shaken, your face is smiled upon, and hopeful, upbeat songs are sung all around you.

Even when the preacher first starts his sermon, things often seem temperate and somewhat reasonable. He reads a passage from the Bible and elucidates at least one possible interpretation of the passage as it relates to being a better person living in the world today. His interpretation is going to be pretty conservative, but that's his prerogative. Slowly, he gets more passionate about the points he is making, most of which have to do with the wrongs he presumes everyone in the congregation has done, as related to the passage. Generally, all these wrong-doings point back to one of the seven deadly sins, with pride really being at the top of the list.

Then, WHAM! He starts banging his fist on the pulpit while his blood pressure spikes. He's yelling, literally shouting, at YOU (always second-person address) about rejecting the call of the Holy Spirit in your life. He's so convinced of your guilt that you begin to wonder. Have you been guilty of the sins he's describing? No, surely not. Or is it your pride and stubbornness that keep you from naming your sins and repenting of them?

That seed of doubt, planted with a massive adrenaline spike from the yelling, gets watered with your tears as the preacher's voice drops to an understanding and compassionate whisper, inviting you to come get right with Jesus, just as a sad, slow song like "Amazing Grace" begins playing. It's hard to realize the emotional trick that has just been played on you. You just got flooded with adrenaline and then had oxytocin dumped into your system. Of course, you need to cry. Of course, you feel an emotional wellspring filling your chest. Of course, you want to go to the front of the church, kneel at the altar, cry your confused and battered heart out, and get praise from everyone present for being so brave and repentant. More hugs follow such repentance. And acceptance. You belong now. Welcome home.

Ugh.

It actually took me years of separation from the church to realize the chemical warfare they played with our body's own neurotransmitters. It's pretty adept brainwashing, really. The day I realized the tricks the preacher was pulling, I wondered if he was systematically taught this process in seminary. Probably not, I conceded. That's just too nefarious, and all these men of God truly believe they are doing good work. To see through the illusion of the format would undoubtedly poke serious holes in the fabric of their faith.

The confetti floating through this parade of emotional manipulation is the single message, "WE are right, righteous, holy, and chosen; while THEY are wrong, evil, and determined to corrupt us." It doesn't matter who THEY are. THEY aren't US. And THEY must be stopped.

The Guardians of Faith didn't disappoint. Women with flowery dresses, big hair, and heavy make-up hugged us while their husbands shook our hands and patted our backs. We got approving looks for the Bibles in our hands, and no less than three different people asked us if this was our first time visiting Guardians of Faith and where our home church was.

"My sister's family and I just moved to town," I lied, indicating Pearl, Robin, and Bea. Then, nodding my head toward Lilly and Evaline, I said, "Our cousins have been looking for a home church in Indianapolis for a while, but nothing really spoke to them until we saw Reverend Sewall speaking on the news. His message

was so stirring. We just knew we had to come check this place out."
Not all lies, I guess.

I scooted us into the back row. The sanctuary was packed
with people of every age. Most were white, I noted. Not sure why
that stood out to me, but it did.

The singing of hymns and collection of offerings happened
without incident. I let the collection plate pass our row without any
of us contributing so much as a hot dime to the cause. The boy
acting as usher scowled at me when I handed him the collection
plate – already full of checks, dollar bills in every denomination,
and children's coins – without adding my own rattle to the
abundance. I pretended not to notice.

The music director left the pulpit and was replaced by
Sewall himself. His greying hair was parted and slick with some
manner of pomade. His black suit looked crisp on his slender
frame, and a golden cross tie-tack stood out against his grey tie. He
looked like a Bush to me, like he could be a cousin of George W.
and Jeb.

"I'd like to welcome you all to the Guardians of Faith
Ministry on this fine Sunday morning," he began. "It's a blessing to
know the Lord is bringing so many of the Faithful to join us for
worship, for fellowship, and for the preparations we all must make
in the fight against evil that faces the city of Indianapolis."

Wow. He didn't waste any time. To my chagrin, this
welcome was met with "Amen" from several members of the
gathered group.

"Let us pray," he continued. "Heavenly Father, we ask that
you be with us today, the day we have set aside each week to
devote to you, filling us with your holy light and girding us with
the armor and protection afforded us in your Scripture. Let us find
refuge and strength in your word, Heavenly Father; and let us not
waver in our commitment as soldiers in your army...."

I could feel all four of my companions shooting nervous and
shocked looks at me. None of us had bowed our heads or folded
our hands, but instead we had all gotten very still during the

minister's prayer. Lilly mouthed the word "soldiers," the question clear in her eyes. "What the fuck?" was her next silent message. I shrugged and looked at the back of the pew in front of me. *Just listen and be cool, ladies. We can talk when we get home.* They couldn't hear my thoughts, but I hoped they would follow my lead.

"… For our city is besieged with iniquity, with sorcery, with the work of the Devil even in this very hour, and we know that it is our duty to carry the Word of your faith into every corner and cast the Devil out. So fortify us, O Lord, as we seek spiritual sustenance. Let your Word be our meat and your Holy Spirit our drink in this, the hour of preparation. We ask these things in your heavenly name. Amen."

A resounding "Amen" echoed from every corner of the sanctuary. Pearl gripped my hand, and I could see from the corner of my eye that we were all holding onto each other. I looked straight ahead and hoped we hadn't made a mistake by coming to this place. The opening prayer is usually pretty light. If he was starting from a place of worry, he was likely to escalate to panic before we got out of this building.

Dr. Thomas Sewall took a deep and steadying breath before looking out over his congregation. He smiled and said, "Witches are among us, my Beloved."

Holy shit.

"The powers and perpetrators of Satan stand poised and ready to devour this city, this state, and this country."

Whew. I mean, yikes. But at least he wasn't about to point to the four women and their shared spirit lover in the back row.

"Satan hates that this is a Christian country," Sewall continued, "and he has convinced so many Americans away from the truth of our foundations. He has told the lie of post-modernism, my Brethren, and so many modern fools have swallowed his deceit, proclaiming it a tasty dish." Muttered agreement from the room. "The lie of post-modernism says that nothing is true except your own experience. It says that what you feel must be right. Satan would have you believe that there are many ways into the

Promised Land, my friends, and using this lie, he will keep you from entering Paradise, if you let him."

Sewall pulled out a slip of paper from amongst his notes and read, "A famous Wiccan author – for the witches who crawl upon their bellies in this post-modern age don't like to name themselves properly… A famous Wiccan author named Scott Cunningham has written in his books that 'It's the highest form of human vanity to assume that your religion is the only way to Deity.'" The reverend paused, letting the message sink in. I could hear clucks and hisses of disapproval. "That's right, my friends. This man would have the young and impressionable people of the world believe that Christians are themselves committing the sins of pride and vanity by simply believing in what Scripture teaches. Did Jesus not say, 'I am the way'?

"A frightening thing has been happening in America in the last few decades. And not just America. It has started in the media, the glamorizing and normalizing of the occult. In the same way that Hollyweird has normalized the abomination of homosexuality – displaying it as a matter of course in television shows and movies until the people are so used to its presence that even the US Supreme Court has corrupted the institution of holy matrimony by allowing homosexuals to marry. In this same way, they have introduced the evils of sorcery and repackaged them so that most people believe they are harmless. They have sanitized the occult through shows like *Sabrina the Teenage Witch*, *Wizards of Waverly Place*, the Harry Potter books and movies; and they have taken something that should horrify us, and they have made it seem harmless to us. We see it as child's play and not the work of the Great Adversary.

"Today, if you wanted to, you could drive just a few blocks down the road and find a New Age shop. Most of you don't know this shop exists, and you likely wouldn't think much about it even if you saw it. In it, they sell stones and greeting cards and jewelry. They burn a little incense and play soothing music. And they lull you into complacency while they steal your soul away from God. It is the message of the New Age – and don't be fooled by that old paganism wrapped in sheep's clothing – that spiritualists, pagans, and even witches are focused on the light. They call themselves light-workers, and they are hoping that you don't know the most famous light-worker of them all – Lucifer. He was highest in the company of Heaven, and his name means 'light-bearer.' And it is the work of that wily serpent to blind mankind with all that glitters and have men perish, believing themselves to be as great as God."

Robin shifted a little in his seat.

"But I tell you today, my friends, that God hates all pagans!" Sewall shouted this anthem. "He hates witches and pagans, and he is very clear about this throughout the Bible.

"Let me turn your attention to the word of God," he said, holding up his black Bible. "Turn with me now to Deuteronomy, chapter 18." He opened to a bookmarked passage. "Starting in verse 10, we read: 'There shall not be found among you anyone that maketh his son or his daughter to pass through the fire, or that useth divination, or an observer of times, or an enchanter, or a witch. Or a charmer, or a consulter with familiar spirits, or a wizard, or a necromancer. For all that do these things are an abomination unto the LORD: and because of these abominations the LORD thy God doth drive them out from before thee.'" He set the book down again, looking at the audience.

"Witchcraft is an abomination to the Lord," he said. "And it is an abomination that has been growing in acceptance and popularity. If we are not careful, we will be at the mercy of idolaters, diviners, charmers, and harlots." He pulled a piece of paper from among his notes and read. "Since 2001, the number of Wiccans has doubled every year. Three out of every four teenagers have engaged in at least one type of psychic or witchcraft-related activity, according to a report in 2006 by George Barna. Three out of every four. Three-quarters of our young people have talked to spirits on a Ouija board, read books about witchcraft, or played video games whose central operations are based on sorcery and spell-casting."

The mothers in the congregation shook their heads and clutched their children tightly to their sides.

"Until a week or so ago," he continued conversationally, "you may have been willing to say that the occult hadn't touched your life, that you hadn't seen any real evidence of witchcraft except in the fantasies of movies and video games. 'What harm is there in the fiction of witchcraft, Brother Sewall?' you might have asked. But it has only been a few short days, my Beloved, since the Devil walked the streets of Indianapolis and claimed a life. That murder was a victory for the old Devil, a victory on two fronts. On the first front, he was able to claim the life of that homeless man, we are told for the purpose of raising a demon of Hell to walk among us. But I tell you that the murdered man is not the only life claimed. The murdering witch, Sondra Little, along with her coven of conspirators are lives and souls that have also been claimed by Satan.

"On the second front, the Devil and his infernal host have claimed – and are still claiming – a victory in the form of those who don't believe that they exist. Even after the proof of Hell's foulness, too many men and women don't believe in the power of the occult. They believe it is make-believe and that witches are not actually capable of magic through their dark arts. But I tell you that the Bible speaks directly about magic and demons and witches. God's word warns of the dangers that can befall us from the occult.

"God condemns enchantment, or the use of magic to make change in the world. We are to rely on him alone." Sewall's volume was starting to rise and his face was reddening. "God condemns the observing of times, astrology, and stargazers. He condemns divination, which is the use of psychics and palm readers and card readers to tell the future. It is only for God to know what path our lives shall take, and no other may know his plans."

Sewall was falling into a cadence. He was practically chanting, I noticed, as he put emphasis on the word "condemns" each time it came around.

79

"God condemns charmers, as well as those who put their faith in charms of luck. It is through God that we reach our goals, as a product of our faith in him. God condemns necromancy, communicating with the dead. God condemns those who call upon familiar spirits. These are demons and spiritual deceivers, preying upon the weak and the hopeless; and God forbids us to soil ourselves with the filth of their presence."

He was shouting properly now. His fist slammed down on the pulpit as he roared, "And God condemns all witches, wizards, and sorcerers. He is clear. 'Suffer not a witch to live,' he tells us."

"Amen" from several men.

"There is a dark power in the world of witchcraft, regardless of the light they claim to seek." He was now pacing along the dais. "Spirits are real, my Brethren. Believe it. The Bible tells us so. And the Devil walks daily in the streets of this and every city looking for whom he may devour."

"Amen."

"We must fight against the forces of Satan!"

"Amen."

"We must protect this city and this nation, proclaiming it once and for all under God's law!"

"Amen."

"We must drive out every vestige of witchcraft from ourselves, from our homes, and from the world!"

"Amen."

"Rid yourself of your good luck charms and your birthday candle wishes, lest God condemn you a charmer. Rid yourself of your daily horoscope and your Farmer's Almanac, lest God see that you rely on signs and not on his true prophecy."

"Amen!"

"Rid yourself of your meditation, martial arts, and yoga, the eastern idolatries that would corrupt your true faith."

"Amen!"

"Rid yourself of the little witchcrafts that you have accepted as harmless, and be a pure and pious child of God." Sewall's volume dropped dramatically. He said softly, but still audibly, "And when you have stripped away the hundreds of little magics that have invaded your life, you will be free to look to God for true guidance on ridding this city, this nation, and this world of the vile stain of witchcraft."

He stopped pacing and ran a hand through his hair. Almost confidentially, he said, "When the Apostle Paul went to Ephesus, he was confronted with a city that relied on the power of magic, though they knew themselves to be believers in the one true God. Every person in that city had little books of magic, little scrolls. Paul showed them, as I have shown you today, that God hates the use of magic. Do you know what the Ephesians did? They burned every book. They burned away all the evil with which they had surrounded themselves, and they were pure and clean once more.

"It's time we burn away evil around us, my friends," he said. "We cannot suffer witchcraft to live within ourselves or within this city. One stands ready for trial today. With God's grace and guidance, all such harlots of the Devil, all such sorcerers and wizards, will be brought to justice, here on earth and in heaven."

"Amen" came booming from all around the room. I looked around myself, no longer transfixed by the minister's terrifying sermon, and I saw that women were crying and several teenage girls were already making their way to the front of the sanctuary as Sewall began the altar call.

I couldn't focus on what little remained of the service. My mind was spinning. Did Dr. Thomas Sewall just call for the burning of witches? In 2016? I think he did.

Holy shit.

Chapter 10

We didn't stay at the church any longer than was absolutely necessary. In fact, we bolted as soon as the closing prayer was finished. We only stayed that long because we didn't want to draw undue attention. I had known the Guardians of Faith were fervent in their beliefs, but now I could see the zeal with which they operated. That sort of zealotry could be dangerous.

It felt dangerous to us. Pearl didn't say a word on the way home, and Lilly kept muttering, "Holy shit," under her breath.

"*Holy* shit, indeed," said Robin, safe inside my house. "*Holy* men like this have tortured and killed cunning men and women all over this globe. I have watched my folk suffer pressing, hanging, burning, and drowning as a part of some *holy* idiot's war. I will not watch that happen to this coven, nor to the cunning folk of this city." He was red with rage, pacing my living room like a large cat.

We sat together, four across, on my sofa. Bea was on Pearl's lap, and we all clung to each other's hands as we had done sitting in that church pew.

"Maybe he was just being metaphorical," I said, the hopeful naiveté of the words making me cringe. Even I didn't believe what I'd just said.

"Oh, no, my love," Robin counselled, "he meant it exactly as you heard it. He may play the politician for a while and have people fooled into thinking he means ideological burning. But if he is able to have his full scheme realized, I believe he would establish burning chambers for the execution of witches, not unlike the gas chamber the reporters say could await Sondra Little if she is convicted of that man's murder. I've seen that much of the man's mind. I can see the fire behind his eyes. In his heart."

"Surely, he could never convince any contemporary legal body to *burn* people, no matter what they are convicted of," said Evaline in horror. "It's so inhumane, so cruel. Most state-sanctioned executions today, where they still exist, are relatively painless."

Robin shook his head. "People are cruel," he said. "And sadistic. And ready to believe any lie they are fed in order to feel both righteous and safe."

Lilly snorted her disgust. "Weapons of mass destruction."

Evaline, Pearl, and I groaned in unison. Robin stared bemusedly at us.

"Several years ago," I explained, "America was attacked by terrorists. So much damage and loss of life. It was unreal. The people who attacked were fanatics, not representative of the countries they were from. But the more conservative elements of our government latched onto these attacks as an excuse to invade Iraq and depose its leader under the premise that they were hiding terrible weapons that could kill even more people."

Robin nodded. "I take it no such weapons were found."

"No," I said. "But we still have military forces there and elsewhere in the Middle East, and we've lost or given up many of our civil liberties here at home in order to feel safer."

Lilly said, "It's like Ben Franklin said, 'They that can give up essential liberty to obtain a little temporary safety deserve neither liberty nor safety.'"

Robin nodded again. "We must fight for both, I think."

Pearl asked, "Are you ready to fight, Robin? Are you able to bring some magical whoop-ass to the fight?"

He considered his answer for a moment. "I will be fully ready soon, I think. Just a few more days if I continue receiving good care at the hands of my witches." His eyes twinkled a little more than I would have thought possible given the gravity of our conversation. Of course, I suppose I would be twinkling, too, if my recovery lay in the beds of my coven sisters, as I very much suspected Robin's recovery did.

Evaline pulled her smartphone out of her pocket and did a quick Google search as she spoke. "There are lots of fronts to fight this war," she said. "We'll need Robin's magical can of whoop-ass soon enough, and we should do whatever spell-work we think will help. But we can also get political, take a stand." She pulled up the website she was seeking and turned the phone's little screen around to face us. "There's a rally happening tomorrow at the courthouse downtown. The Indy Wiccan-Pagan Alliance are organizing it, along with the local interfaith ministers group. They're going to hand out flyers saying what witchcraft is and what it isn't, and they are going to show both local and national media that we can all play nice and take a reasonable approach to this horrible situation."

I looked at the screen, committing the details of time and place to memory. "I take it you're planning on going?"

She nodded.

"I will also go with you," Robin volunteered. "I had hoped to spend a few days at your residence, Evaline, if that is acceptable?"

She blushed just a little. Evaline was very private about her sexual encounters. She must have known that we would all assume they were having sex if he stayed in her one bedroom bungalow in Bloomington. The pattern was already pretty clear.

"Space is at a premium," she said, "but you're welcome to crash on my couch."

Nah. I wasn't buying it. She could be as private as she liked. I could feel the tension between them. When Evaline thought no one was paying attention to her, she looked at Robin like he was a chew toy and she was ready to play.

He smirked as he replied, "I will be delighted with whatever space you permit to me." And he winked. Well, not quite a wink. More like an eyelid twitch followed by a gleam.

Private as she was, Evaline didn't give ground. She didn't break his gaze, and she didn't blush this time. Not even a little. She also didn't escalate this minor sexual drama by issuing a challenge or playing coy. "You are an honored guest of this coven, Magister. My home, like those of my sisters, is yours."

"Gramercy," he said, with a tilt of his head.

"Whoa, get a room, you two," Pearl interjected, pretending to fan herself. "I can't take it after that Sewall non-sense today. My blood pressure just keeps spiking. Y'all can save all that tension for the foreplay."

"Indeed," Robin said with another wink. This one was definitely a wink, and it was aimed at Pearl. "So, Miss Pearl, will you be joining Evaline and myself at the assembly on the courthouse lawn tomorrow morning?"

"No, I can't," she said. "I have to work. Daily life calls. Accountants gotta account."

"What about you, Lilly?" Evaline asked. "Should I pick you up on the way there?"

"I wish I could, but I'm working a double tomorrow," Lilly sighed. "Marni took off again, and the rest of us are scrambling to cover her shifts. I'm sure the boss is going to fire her this time. I don't care how many blow jobs she's thrown his way, he can't overlook this one."

We all knew about Lilly's roommate. They waited tables together at a "gentlemen's show club" on Pendleton Pike. Sometimes Marni danced. She had been wanting to dance more, and Lilly suspected she was turning tricks after hours. Lilly also suspected Marni was messing with drugs heavier than the weed she'd smoked when Lilly first moved in with her.

"You've got to move out of there," I said. "I worry about you. You could come move in with me and Grace. We can make space for you."

Lilly shrugged. "Maybe. Monrovia is awfully far from work."

I knew she made excellent tips at the strip club. Hell, Lilly made better money than some of the dancers. She was strikingly pretty, charming, intelligent, and a damn good waitress. She would sit with the customers to take their orders and flirt mercilessly with them. She made lewd jokes and sexy innuendos. I'm not sure if she gave the men the same "might score" impression that the more alluring dancers gave, or if they saw slightly naughty girlfriend material in her. Whatever it was, they tipped her better than she could hope to make working at Chili's.

"Might be worth it," I said. "Just keep thinking about it. I don't trust Marni, and I trust her friends even less. I want you to be safe, and I don't want you to be robbed blind by your roommate."

Lilly laughed. "Oh, she knows better than to mess with me. I helped her out of a sticky situation with her boyfriend a few months back. She helped me get some of the ingredients for the goofer dust I used to send him packing."

Yikes. "You didn't do something nasty to him with a muggle looking on, did you?"

"No," Lilly said with a cat-like grin. "I just made him leave town. If you're worried about my reputation, don't. I'm pretty certain crack whores aren't considered any more reputable than witches. Overall, I'm much more reputable than Marni."

"Do you really think she's a crack whore?" I asked. "That's pretty harsh."

Lilly shrugged. "I hope it's not crack, but she's trading herself for some kind of high."

"Do people still use the term 'strawberry?' I can't say it without thinking of the movie *Pretty Woman*," I said.

"So, the rally," Evaline interjected, her eyebrows arched. I guess Lilly and I had gotten pretty far off topic. "Lilly and Pearl can't make it. What about you and Grace?"

"I should be able to meet you there," I said. "I can mention it to Grace, but I am sure she'll decline. She is pretty freaked out about all of this. She had a terrible panic attack last night when we were making plans for today's church visit." I lowered my voice. "You've probably noticed she hasn't come out of her room, either. I know she can hear that we're home. I honestly just hope she isn't in there having another episode by herself."

Lilly shook her head. "I don't even know if you should mention the rally to her. I don't think she can handle it."

Pearl arched an eyebrow. "So we can't even talk with her about the fact that the ass-hat wants to burn witches in Indianapolis? I mean, aren't we at the time and place when we *should* panic? And then after a little panic, we should stop this bullshit. How is not talking about it going to make it any better?"

I nodded. I felt my mouth twist. That's the look I make when I have a whole lot to say and don't think most of it would be productive. I agreed with Pearl. Completely. The trouble was that I knew Grace. She was shutting down on this topic. No amount of logic would make her see reason. No stirring speech would prompt her into action.

In fact, she had a tendency to feel assaulted by logic and harassed by stirring speeches when she was in this type of mood. Her moribund sobbing had a way of convincing the deliverer of said logic and speeches that they were abusing her. You felt like you were beating a defenseless child, not having an adult conversation.

None of that would be helpful to say right now. Evaline had never witnessed this side of Grace. Pearl tended to be unsympathetic to most emotional extremes, even of her closest friends. Lilly and Robin were fairly neutral, and they were close enough to see for themselves, if indeed there was anything to see. With any luck, we could get through this crisis without putting undue strain on tender Gracie.

Chapter 11

There are more pagans and witches in Indianapolis than you'd think. Hell, there are more in my little bedroom community than you might guess. I know of at least three, not counting Grace and me. She had met several when she worked at the local library before making the move to give tarot readings in Indy. A library patron would recognize her triskelion necklace or the Goddess charm on her bracelet and ask in hushed tones if she was like them. A pagan.

The code, before our time, had been to ask, "Are you in the *family*?" If the person in question looked confused and asked which family you meant, you could always play it off like you thought they were a second cousin you had seen at last year's reunion. If they knowingly said that yes, yes they were in the *family*, you both knew you'd found a brother or sister witch. Anyone overhearing this exchange thought nothing about it.

Because witchcraft had come so far into the light of day, into a tentative public acceptance, this custom and the caution it bespoke have been all but lost. Now that we are feeling a little heat again, we are caught midway between the broom closet and the courthouse lawn. Hundreds of us were standing together with local ministers of liberal denominations. Hundreds of us. That was a thousand less than I saw at our last Pagan Pride Day.

Most of the time you can't tell a witch from a Baptist or a Catholic or a Mormon by her clothes. We look like soccer moms and dentists and attorneys and telemarketers because that's exactly what we are. Well, some of us. Others are a little more non-traditional in both profession and appearance. Psychics, herbalists, midwives, and life coaches sporting shawls and fringe and patchwork. A few of the "witches" assembled at the courthouse were wearing pointy hats and cloaks, leaning on tall staffs with crystals on the ends. These folks always made me groan a little. I never knew if they were real adherents of the old ways who were also very flamboyant and silly, or if they were mildly delusional, socially awkward coots who simply reveled in being odd.

We had the whole spectrum out for the rally. I was making my way from the table of free coffee to where I saw Robin and Evaline. My progress was slow, as friends I normally only saw once or twice a year at Pagan Pride and the annual charity ball said hello and gave me hugs.

Robin and Evaline were in the thick of the crowd, very near a loud woman in her late-fifties who was directing the show. She was holding a sign that read "Harm None." Two other women about her age were passing signs out to newcomers. I knew the leader from the local shop I use for hard-to-find spell supplies.

"Alright everyone," she shouted to the assembled group. "I want to thank all of you for coming out to support the Indy Wiccan Alliance and the Heartland InterFaith Ministers Coalition in showing the media and the justice system who we are."

There was only one news crew on hand today, it seemed. I guess a plea for peace and reason isn't as newsworthy as a sensational murder.

"We are joined by Allison Sheffield of the Covenant of Solitaires, the group to which Sondra Little belongs," the rally leader explained. "Together, we can show this city, this state, and this country that Wiccans are peaceful, productive, non-violent members of this and every community in the U.S. The central ethical belief in Wicca is the Rede. It says, 'An it harm none, do what thou wilt.' A Wiccan wouldn't murder. A Wiccan doesn't do harm. Our local police need to look elsewhere for their murderers. Sondra Little is innocent."

She started the chant of "harm none" as the assembled crowd pumped their signs in the air. My covenmates, I noticed, did not have signs that echoed the chant, and I knew why. Their sign said, "Free Sondra Little." I was signless.

Evaline and Robin didn't have "harm none" signs because most traditional witches find the Wiccan Rede to be a little fluffy. It's a sweet sentiment, and it serves as a good starting point for evaluating your own ethics. We certainly don't believe, for example, that an ethical witch would actively seek to harm another person for her own personal gain. But we try to be honest with ourselves about the ramifications of all our actions, both magical and mundane. Someone at my old office got a promotion because I was fired. Does that make that person unethical? No, of course not. What if they prayed really hard to get a promotion just before I got fired? I am most certainly harmed by being unemployed, but it isn't my replacement's fault. What if, instead of praying, my replacement had done a spell? Since spells are basically just active prayers, you can't claim the magic was any more unethical than the prayer.

This example is relatively benign, but you can probably see where it would get tricky with things like prosperity spells that take form by grandma dying and leaving you an inheritance. Most witches of my coven's ilk see the Rede as an attempt to wash a witch's hands of responsibility for an unexpected outcome. We generally face our responsibilities head-on by doing some divination to see what sort of sacrifice or exchange is needed for the magic at hand.

All magic comes at a price. Energy moves in waves. There is an ebb and flow to it. A balance. More of something here means less of something there. The universe maintains its own balance, and very often a witch is already in touch with the flow. When she's not, and she wants to perform a bit of magic that creates a bigger ripple in the pond than was expected, there is a sacrifice to be made. She can make that sacrifice before she does her spell, or the universe can take it from her however it sees fit later. But there is always a price.

Sounds like sacrifice, yes? You're right, it is. But here's the caveat about sacrifice: It isn't a sacrifice if it doesn't cost you something dear to pay it. You have to feel it. You have to need the thing so badly that you are willing to give up something you value to get it. Your blood is your life force. That is one of the most potent sacrifices you can make. It doesn't take much, though. A few drops, at most. One drop of blood contains your entire genetic code. You don't have to spill a bucket. And it has to be yours, given freely. It costs you nothing to spend someone else's money, nor does a stranger's blood satisfy the need for sacrifice. Not within witchcraft, at least.

This is why I was so sure that Sondra Little was innocent. For one thing, she probably believed in the Rede so ardently that she wouldn't have hurt a fly if it meant winning the lottery. For another, being a witch alone meant that she'd probably never even been taught about the need for sacrifice in the books on Wicca she'd purchased from the local shops. The shopkeepers tend to keep their books and wares as non-threatening to the general public as possible. The idea of sacrifice, especially blood sacrifice, has been so misrepresented through the ages that it just isn't discussed among non-initiates.

The final thing that told me Sondra Little was innocent was the nature of the sacrifice itself. Yes, I know that human sacrifice – the offering up of another person's life, another person's blood, another human being's spark – has happened in the past. Yes, I fully understand that the demon being summoned by the woman in the picture is quite pleased with the killing of that poor homeless man. But it isn't because she sacrificed in the way witches do. No. It is because she has sacrificed her own purity to do this thing. She has stained herself by cruelly taking his life. She has marred her own soul. That is price she is paying. Sondra Little, the mousy pre-school teacher *cum* solitary witch, doesn't seem at all capable of paying that price.

Evaline spotted me through the crowd and waved me closer. I'd almost made it to where she and Robin stood when a voice boomed across a loudspeaker. Reverend Sewall had arrived on the scene, along with a portable amplifier and microphone, two more news crews, and no less than two hundred of his followers.

"Indianapolis demands justice," he shouted. His projected voice drowned out the stunned chanters. "You cannot spread your lies and your filth here. We have seen the *harm* done by witches in the photos the authorities received. We have felt the *harm* of witchcraft and magic creeping into our children's lives, their entertainment. You would have our young people buy into your pagan propaganda and get Harry Potter to waive his magic wand to help them with their troubles instead of falling to their knees in prayer and seeking the aid of Jesus Christ."

I blinked. What?

"The law enforcement personnel of this city have PROOF that it was Sondra Little, a known WITCH, who committed the heinous ritual murder," Sewall continued, relying more on the passion of his conviction than any rational proof available to the police or anyone else. "Sondra Little and at least two other members of her coven did this, and the *good people* of Indianapolis won't sit idly by any longer."

One man among the rally participants shouted, "But she was a solitary. She wasn't in a coven."

Sewall didn't hear him, or pretended not to hear him. He held up a small stack of papers in his gloved hand. "I have here a petition to the lawmakers of this God-fearing state, signed by no less than two-thousand men and women, demanding the outlaw of witchcraft in the state of Indiana. That's two-thousand Indianapolis Christians, Jews, and Muslims signing in the last three days who want to see the liberal laws protecting witches repealed immediately. We're going to be working hard to get that number up to 60,000 in the next couple of weeks. That's just 1% of our population, folks; but it should be enough to get the repeal of witchcraft protections into the hands of our law-makers. And then we will be free from the pernicious ministrations of diviners and necromancers. Free from the spell-casters who would most certainly *harm* us, if given the chance. "

Sewall's people cheered and shouted.

"But we aren't stopping there!" he escalated. "No, we mustn't stop there. It isn't enough to clap the witches into a jail cell for their deceit and devilry. No. Ones like this Miss Little, ones who have committed horrific murder under the auspices of idolatry and hellish intentions, these harlots of the devil must suffer swift and fearful punishment for their crimes. We must not suffer the witch to live."

As if in cue, his followers took up the cry "Suffer not the witch!"

Well, holy shit.
Again.

Chapter 12

She took a long, deep drag from her vape pen. Pointless as she knew it was, she actually wished she had a real cigarette in her hands. The glowing tip of a bona fide cigarette had always given her the illusion of warmth on cold days. Autumn was setting in, and Indianapolis could be a frigid bitch even in the early fall.

Her "date" should be arriving soon to pick her up. She laughed to herself. *Date?* She couldn't remember the last john who had even bought her a meal.

Even so, she made more money as an escort than she did as a waitress. Even working the pole was shitty money compared to turning tricks. With the wide world of technology being what it is, she didn't even have to freeze her sweet little ass off every night walking 10th Street. She didn't have to take out expensive ads in magazines, either. She could just post her offer on craigslist, and she was sure to get calls.

Her boyfriend had turned her onto hooking. *Ex*-boyfriend. She didn't need his ass. That abusive, controlling dick. "I can be your protection, baby. Make sure you come home safe from making that money." Yeah, right. *I don't need a goddam pimp, taking my money and beating me up.* The first time he hit her was the last. She gave him the boot and went back to the club, punching that clock for a few weeks. She made him believe she was done with him and done with tricks until he lost interest.

Far from done, she was developing grand plans. She'd met a couple other girls on some of her dates. You'd be shocked what type of business advice a working girl can get on the fly. On the job training. One girl had pointed her in the direction of a couple of blogs written by call girls about the business. She had her sights set on real money. Like, "$500 every time she spread her legs" kind of money.

This was her first date at her new price. She wasn't asking $500 for tonight, but she was trying out the $200 per hour price point. And she had a taker.

The car pulled up outside the bar she used for Wednesday night hook-ups. She had learned to alternate between a few locations. She always had a drink or two, tipped nicely, and chatted up the bartender. She took another drag from her vape pen and waved like she actually knew the man behind the tinted glass.

He got out and walked around to her side, opening the door for her. *Oh, my! This might be like a real date after all.* She smiled to herself. *They treat you better when you charge a little more. Wonder how well I'll be treated when I'm charging $500 for an hour of my goodies.*

He got back in the car. He seemed nervous. Sweaty. Clammy, actually. He readjusted his grip on the steering wheel. His shoulders slouched a little under his raincoat, and he sported dark circles under his pouchy eyes. His thick, soft lips seemed to tremble. *Is this his first time with a hooker?*

"So, honey," she broke the ice, "I'm awfully glad you called me for a date. You seem like a sweetie. I bet we're going to have a lot of fun together."

He didn't say anything but shot a quick glance behind her into the back seat where another woman was silently watching her.

"Fucking Christ, lady!" she said. "You almost scared me to death. I didn't hear you back there."

The woman in the back didn't say a word. She drew her finger to her lips as if to say "hush."

Okay, she thought to herself, *I don't know what kind of kinks this fella is into, but if he can afford both of us, I'll just play along. I bet she's charging a pretty penny tonight, too. That's an awfully snazzy red dress.*

Chapter 13

"I can't be here," Lilly shrieked. "I can't be in this apartment. Not now."

Her eyes were wild and her breathing was ragged. She'd been pacing and screaming obscenities when Pearl and I arrived. Clothes and makeup were tossed messily into a bag with a sketchbook and a half-finished crochet project. I thought I saw a couple of amber colored bottles floating around in there, too. I'd ask her what they were later.

"The police were here, Rose," she said, every word a strain. "They asked me questions about Marni. They … they showed me the picture of what those animals did to her." She shuddered, hard. "I've never had a panic attack before, not like Grace does. But, Rose, I completely lost it." She shook her head, trying to shake away the image that I was sure would stick with her the rest of her life. "I didn't like her much, and she was a lousy roommate, but holy fucking hell. What they did to her was so awful."

I had no idea what to say. None. Emily Post never suggested the proper etiquette for talking to your understandably freaked out coven sister upon the discovery of her prostitute roommate's brutal murder at the hands of psychopathic occultists.

"Can I make you a cup of tea?" I offered. It probably wasn't the right response, but it was my go-to.

Lilly just stared at me for a moment, expressionless. I thought she was going to yell again, which I would have understood. "Sure," she said.

We moved to the kitchen, and I started the ritual of putting the kettle on.

Pearl sat next to Lilly on the bar stool on the other side of the pass-through window. "What did the police say?" she asked.

"Not much, really," Lilly said. "They showed me the picture and asked if the woman in it was Marni Wilson. They asked me when I last saw her. I told them it had been a few days, but that wasn't really unusual for Marni. They asked if I was aware of her activities as a prostitute and whether I knew who she was meeting last night."

"What did you tell them?" Pearl asked.

"The truth," Lilly said simply. "I knew Marni had picked up a drug habit, and I had suspected she might be having sex for money, drugs, or both. But Marni never confided any of that to me, and she sure as hell didn't involve me with her clientele."

"Did they come into the apartment?" I asked. I was looking at a row of novena spell candles set inside a colorful shrine. The items might look like ethnic chatchkes to an uneducated person, but ethnic flair looks a lot like sorcery during a witch panic.

"No," she said with breathy emphasis. "They suggested maybe coming in to talk, but I knew better. I told them I was tired from working a double last night, covering Marni's hours, actually. I asked if I could talk to them later today, after I'd had a chance to rest and clean up a little."

"I'm surprised they didn't have a warrant," Pearl said.

"Me, too, kind of," Lilly replied. "But I'm grateful they didn't."

"I guess none of us really knows much about police procedures aside from what we've seen on tv crime dramas," I said. "Maybe they didn't have one for the apartment yet because it isn't actually a crime scene."

Lilly shrugged. "I don't know. I figure it doesn't matter too much. They will likely come back with one. When they do, I intend to have my personal sundries, including anything that could look like witchcraft, packed up and out of here."

I poured water from the now-whistling tea pot into the only mug I could find. It was a funky lion cup circa 1973. The handle was the lion's tail. I swear the poor lion looked pained.

"We can help you get your things packed up, sister," I said as I handed her the lion mug. "And since you're not taking everything, it shouldn't look too bare. Where all do you have your magical items?"

Her eyes wandered aimlessly. "Mostly my bedroom. A couple here, obviously," she said, nodding at the little kitchen altar. "Maybe a charm in the bathroom, but I don't know if it would look like magic to anyone who doesn't know what it is already."

Luckily, Lilly had mostly been very stealthy about her magic. She had other roommates before Marni, none of whom she fully trusted. She had a latch on her bedroom door with a padlock. We'd leave it open for the police, because Lilly didn't need to rouse their suspicions any more than possible. But that latch was always locked when she wasn't home.

Her bedroom didn't look like just a touch of ethnic flair. It looked like the lair of a voodoo queen. After we bagged up the small animal skulls, the small dark bottles of oils, the mojo bags, and the creepy dolls, though, it looked like the bedroom of your average Goth cocktail waitress. A little on the dark side, but not alarmingly so.

Figuring out space in our house for Lilly wasn't going to be a problem. There were three bedrooms on the main floor of the house and three more in the basement. One of the basement rooms was our temple space. One was our library. We were book whores, so the library was the largest of the basement rooms, with shelves lining the walls and books lining the shelves. A squashy wing-back chair occupied the center of the room with a floor lamp at its side. The final basement bedroom was our craft workshop. The rest of the space downstairs was a very unused dance studio "slash" workout room. Grace and I had big ideas about starting a belly dance tribe, but we didn't really know other dancers, and Grace was less graceful than her name would suggest.

Upstairs were both of our bedrooms and a spare room we tried to keep tidy for overnight guests. Tried. It was often the junk room. We spent an hour whisking the junk to its many rightful locations throughout the house, and Lilly started the process of settling in. It only took another hour for Lilly's new room to look like it, too, had been inhabited by Marie Leveau.

Around six o'clock, Lilly emerged and switched on the television. "I've got to see what they're saying about this," she said.

Grace excused herself to her bedroom, giving Lilly a quick hug as she went. She said, her voice full of sympathy, "I understand why you need to see. I hope you can understand why I can't."

Lilly nodded and patted Grace on the arm before turning her attention to the opening of the newscast.

"Tonight's top story: Indianapolis woman suspected of prostitution is slain in the city's second ritual homicide." Footage with the words "recorded live earlier today" began rolling. Marshall Vance, the police chief, once again read a prepared statement.

"We are disappointed to report that another victim of an occult-related homicide was discovered early this morning on the city's west side in an abandoned home. The murders seem to be connected, as both victims were displayed in a similar position with the same symbol imprinted upon their bodies. The federal Behavioral Analysis Unit is assisting local police in the investigation by preparing profiles on the possible individuals involved in these murders. We believe a group, or coven, *of men and women are behind these atrocities, and we are working diligently to apprehend those responsible and bring peace back to the Circle City."*

The telecast switched back to the grim-faced anchor. *"Tensions are mounting here in the Heartland as the second ceremonial-style murder is committed here in Indianapolis. Church groups and concerned individuals are expressing the fear that a murderous coven of witches is to blame."*

The disembodied voice of a female reporter spoke over a picture of the strip club where Lilly worked. *"Marni Wilson, age 24, was a cocktail waitress and dancer at this west side night club. She was last seen by her co-workers five days ago, leaving the club to meet a friend. Her body was found this morning, police say, after an anonymous tip led them to an abandoned home near Lafayette Square on the city's west side.*

"*While that area of town has had a long history of gang- and drug-related violence, officials are looking for members of a different sort of group.*" A series of several images presented a slideshow of witchcraft. An altar with pentagram and candles, the logos of local and national witchcraft organizations, the close-up shot of the three red-robed and hooded participants of the last murder, the sigil of the demon. "*Witchcraft has been legal in the US and UK since the mid-1950's, though laws related to fraud and the unlicensed practice of medicine have often kept witchcraft-related practices like fortune-telling and herbalism confined. In the last several years, witches have practiced their arts more openly, claiming theirs is a peaceful, nature-based religion whose adherents are taught not to harm others in their pursuit of a magical life.*" The last image in the slide-show was taken at the rally, and it featured Robin and Evaline front and center, flanked by the bossy witch and one of her helpers. I couldn't breathe. All the color drained out of Lilly's face.

The camera clicked over to the live image of the reporter whose voice we'd been hearing. Sewall was at her side. "*I'm joined this evening by Rev. Thomas Sewall, of the Guardians of Faith Ministries, an outspoken detractor of the pro-witchcraft movement. Rev. Sewall, can you tell me why you believe all witches, not just those earning their livings through the magical arts, should be documented?*"

"*Thank you, Leslie,*" he smiled. "*If we look at witchcraft historically, in the early American colonies, in Europe, and around the globe, we see a distinct pattern of violence and human sacrifice. While the most vocal proponents of Wicca depict themselves as law-abiding citizens, we can see, as evidenced by these recent atrocities, that brutality and inhumanity are at the rotten heart of the witches' beliefs. To keep our God-fearing, truly law-abiding citizens safe, we need to know who the witches are in our neighborhoods, in our offices, and in our government.*"

The reporter asked, "*So, you're recommending an expansion of the OPRA index to include all witches. How do you propose these individuals be identified, if they are hesitant to register themselves?*"

"*I believe that a competent council could be trained to hear and evaluate evidence from a variety of anecdotal sources,*" he said mildly, as if he weren't suggesting a New Inquisition. *"It is my experience that most witches are known to their neighbors, their co-workers, and their family members. If they are truly adherents of the laws, if they are undeniably moral in their behavior, then I see no reason why these men and women would be hesitant to speak openly and truthfully about their beliefs. We are facing a new crisis in this country. We have faced, as a nation, the threat of communism in the mid-twentieth century and won. We have faced the threat of terrorism in the early twenty-first century, and we have won. We have preserved America because our citizens have been willing to make the hard choices, to name those who posed the greatest threat to their safety and security. We now face the threat of occult terrorism, and we must once again win."*

Was the reporter startled by the minister's call to arms? I couldn't quite tell. She had hitched her "neutral news correspondent" face in place. *"Dr. Sewall, your organization is also petitioning the State to institute a policy of execution-by-fire in the case of Sondra Little if she is found guilty. Is that accurate?"* She was speaking through tense jaws.

"Yes, Leslie," he replied in somber tones. *"It is a gruesome punishment that is befitting the crime in this case. Traditionally, witches have been burned at the stake as atonement for their sins. But there may have been other reasons, too, that our forebears understood better than we do today. They believed in the power of the witch, but that belief was suppressed for generations. We allowed witches to disappear into the quiet and dark shadows, and we punished those claiming small displays of witchcraft power as frauds and charlatans. Some were merely frauds, and their corresponding penalties – fines and jail time – were appropriate to their crimes. But we have seen that witchcraft power is real. We have seen it working in the world. The fire, and only the fire, will bring an end to the devilish work of the witch."*

Reporter Leslie took a breath as she turned back to the camera. *"Back to you in the studio."*

I clicked the tv off.

"Goddammit! Why do they have to keep showing that symbol? It's giving that beast power that he shouldn't be allowed to have," I was up and pacing.

"They don't know that, though," Lilly said. "They don't know anything about how this works. That last bit about the fire was wrong, wasn't it?" She was pale.

I sat down, my hands gripped tight. "Yeah, I've never heard or read anything like that before. I don't think it's true. I think burning witches is just a way to exact a measure of vengeance and cruelty in the name of the law."

We sat in silence for a moment. There was so much to hash through. Evaline's face was on the news as a participant in a witchcraft-related protest. I had already been fired on allegations related to the craft. Lilly's roommate had been savagely murdered by some nasty occultists, and she was going to be terrifyingly close to this investigation. Too close for any witch to feel comfortable. Lilly obviously wasn't involved, and she had a solid alibi. She had been at work covering Marni's shift. Of course, I thought it was pretty obvious that Sondra Little hadn't been involved in the first murder, but the police were still holding her.

And now Sewall was doing his damnedest to stir up a massive witch hunt. We could probably have taken steps to quell the witch craze from ever taking root, if only that other coven – whoever they were – would stop killing the indigent people of Indianapolis.

Chapter 14

I hated going back to the courthouse lawn. After seeing Evaline's face on the news and hearing Sewall's hate-filled, registry-promoting rhetoric, I felt unsafe, exposed. But if Evie was willing to go back, I would go with her. We had to stand up for our basic civil rights. We couldn't expect the muggles to protect us. We had to do that ourselves. And that meant fighting back against vocal assholes who wanted us punished for our beliefs. It meant being seen as real people, not as the boogey-women of childhood nightmares.

The bossy Wiccan from the last protest had been arrested. Sarah "Star" Gould owned a small magical shop on the near-west side. Earth-Star Mercantile, she called it. She had run it for years, teaching Wicca 101 and running a local Wicca-based charity that provided gently used coats and a bit of a food pantry for her neighborhood. Everyone involved in the Craft in Indianapolis knew Star. We all went to her for the essentials that you couldn't pick up in a health food store and you didn't trust from online suppliers.

Most of her shop was filled with vaguely-witchy knickknacks and jewelry that were on consignment from local artists and "Crafters." Witches like making things. There's more than one reason we call it the "Craft."

Everyone knew Star, but none of us thought she was capable of this murder. She was bossy and a little brash, but she was one of the most ardent adherents to the Rede that I'd ever met. She wouldn't sell items that had a reputation for negative magic, even if you could use them in a more positive way, as well. On a good day, she would educate you about the correct way to handle the problem. Her correct way, of course. One that was very light-filled and gentle. "Bless them and send them on their way," I'd heard her say. On a fussy day, she would send you out of the store with a warning not to come back until you were walking the right-hand path. She's never done this to me or anyone I know, but I'd heard rumors.

I had never taken her Wicca 101 class. For one thing, I was well past the 101 level when I moved to Indianapolis. For another, I'm not Wiccan. I admired the openness of Wicca and the political strides they had made for the Pagan community, but I found Wicca lacking a certain amount of grit. It was detached from the history of witchcraft, the history that showed witches using magic to defend themselves, their homes, families, and livelihoods. It was detached from the reality of witches using their magic to earn a living. Most Wiccans, Star included, believe it is immoral for a witch to charge a price for her magic – including teaching skills to newbies. You could only charge for a product, a physical item in your hand, according to Star.

I had never been taught those rules, and I didn't find value in them now. No, I wasn't earning my living as a witch. Not yet, at least. But I saw no problem with charging a client for a tarot reading, charging a student for a class, or charging a petitioner for a spell. If a person comes to me with a problem that they don't have the skill or knowledge to solve, and they've tried the other avenues available to them, I would do the spell if I felt like the work itself was in line with my own ethics. But magic always comes with a price. That price can be paid with cash – the survival credits we all use in this crazy multi-player game of life.

Star and both of her worker bees were arrested, along with Star's husband. The police had announced that they had apprehended the coven they believed were responsible for both murders. Sondra Little, they said, had clear connections to Sarah Gould and the witchcraft ring she operated from her store. They had reason to believe that this coven had perpetrated both murders.

They weren't releasing any more details until they had concluded their investigation.

Utter bullshit.

So, here I was with Robin and Evie amidst a worried and agitated group of witches at the courthouse. This wasn't a rally for interfaith cooperation. This was a protest. We all knew the police had the wrong people. Star's coven couldn't have done this.

We weren't alone in our demonstration. The Guardians of Faith were also there, clamoring for a swift trial for all five of the arrested Wiccans. A swift trial and a torturous execution.

Nobody from our side was in costume today. I was grateful for that. I was also grateful that more of us came out to show support for the Earth-Star Five. I hated the moniker, but I wasn't exactly in charge of PR.

Our biggest issue, aside from the Guardians of Faith being hateful zealots just a few yards away, was our lack of leadership. Star had been the vocal leader of our last public gathering, and nobody seemed keen on taking her place. Either nobody knew what to do or say, or they were all too afraid to speak up.

A few people had signs. Nothing catchy or clever was on any of them. That was a shame. I mean, the word "spell" as it relates to magic is tied to the idea of writing or speaking words of power. Chanting is tied up with enchantment. And what do protesters do if not chant?

I had an idea. It was a simple idea, but it could prove to be a shocking one. Sewall and his minions were already making a lot of noise. The minister was already into one of his rants. I knew it wouldn't be long before they started in with "Suffer not the witch" again. I wanted my people to get the drop on them. I wanted us to do what we do.

I turned my back to Sewall, and I raised my voice loud enough for the throng of witches near me to hear it. I knew the idea would get telegraphed to the outliers pretty quickly once we got started.

"These are scary times, folks," I started. "But not in the way that those hate-mongers would have everyone believe. These are scary times because hate and fear are being encouraged to thrive. Dr. Sewall is fanning the flames of that fear. We need to quench that fire before it burns us all down. We need to show the world that we are not what they fear. We need to help them see that the people they have in jail right now are innocent."

The twinkle in Robin's eyes was evident as he pitched the proverbial soft ball. "What do you suggest we do?"

I looked at the crowd. "I suggest we raise power and send it toward our goal." I spoke louder so even the folks at the far edges of the crowd could hear. "Our intent is to bring calm clarity to our law-makers and law-enforcers. Let them move forward without fear, without hate, and pursue the real criminals behind these murders. Let us clasp hands and chant. Let us raise power and send calm clarity to the police force, the judges, and the legislature. Are we of one mind?"

The crowd replied with a single voice, "We are."

"Make circles within circles, all moving clockwise," I said. I quickly explained the pattern we would be using – three turns around the circle, followed by a quarter-turn back. The traditional witches knew this technique. The Wiccans didn't. I made sure one or two people in each circle knew what to do and were willing to lead.

We were all set and ready when it struck me. Shit. What were we going to chant? I looked at Evaline, panic bare on my face. She winked and opened her mouth to sing a simple tune. "We tread the mill to quench the fire that Justice won't burn on the pyre." When the words and turn had filtered out to the gathered witches and we were all singing in unison, Evaline held up her hand for silence. "And there's a descant, if you're up for it." She sang a slower verse with a haunting tune. "Earth, flame, sea, air – This is our prayer." We sang that a few times until the crowd had it, too.

I nodded at Evie and Robin, and we started moving. "We tread the mill to quench the fire that Justice won't burn on the

106

pyre." It was a haunting tune. We used the same basic tune all the time in our coven for spell work, but I'd never sung it with over a hundred other voices before. It was eerie and beautiful.

And the circles! All those people treading the mill of magic in unison. Except it wasn't exactly in unison. There were five concentric circles that all started at the same pace, all moving clockwise. But the inner, small circles didn't take as long to walk three times around their short circumference. As they treaded back the few paces, there was a ripple effect with the second circle and then the third, moving counter clockwise for a short time. Soon, there was always at least one circle moving opposite the others, the pattern almost indistinguishable to the eye. It was dizzying. I had to focus just on what my circle was doing or I would fall down.

I could feel the energy rising. My face was warm, and the hairs on my arms and neck were standing. I could feel Sewall's group watching us. I could feel the weight of their shock and silence. I'm not sure that they imagined we would actually do witchcraft in front of them on the courthouse steps.

The energy washed over us, spiraled around us all. If the visual pattern of the five circles was complex, the music had become no less so. Without verbally communicating to each other what we would do, the main line of the verse was being sung in rounds by three of the circles. The other two were singing only the descant. Those who could harmonize, did. And at least two people, neither of whom I could see, were drumming. I momentarily wondered who thought to bring African djembes to a protest, but then I let it go. Witches.

We were loud, I think. But the music seemed soft to me. I focused on my circle, on keeping my feet moving in the right direction, on singing my part of the song. I felt strong, and I could see that strength in the other members of my circle. Inner strength. A strength that didn't have to thump its chest or snarl to be seen and heard.

Through our chant, I thought I heard Sewall's voice rise up in attempted anger. He was trying to whip his followers into a fury again. Trying to get them to start their own chant, but the few who tried gave up. Their cacophony echoed back to them, the discordance of their message unable to stand while we chanted. I heard him call for his followers to pray and not to be swayed by the work of the devil. And then I only heard us. Lovely, hallowing, hair-raising us.

I'm not sure how much time passed. Twenty minutes. Two hours. However long it had been, I started feeling the pressure of the rising energy. It was nearing its peak. It demanded that we speed our pace, both with our feet and with our words. We obeyed.

We were nearly running in our circles, almost tripping over our boots and sneakers, the chant spilling out of our mouths so quickly it was impossible to hear the individual words. And then BAM! We all stopped at once, flung our hands skyward and shouted ululations to the heavens. The energy sped away from us toward its goal. I lifted my face and shouted, "As we will it, so mote it be." Then with more emphasis, "As we will it ...."

The crowd responded, "... so mote it be."

"By the power of three times three ...," I said.

Together, "As we will it, so mote it BE."

Chapter 15

I was fuzzy after the public spell work downtown. I hadn't brought food to ground out the last of the energy or to replenish my own flagging levels. I know I was interviewed. I should have anticipated that before I opened my mouth to talk to the crowd. Don't know if it would have made me hesitate or not. Probably not.

I was not crazy about my name being publicly linked to both witchcraft and this case. If Sewall got his way, I would not be able to avoid his damned registry. Everyone in the city would know I was a witch as soon as the evening news aired.

Let it go, I told myself. *Just showing up on that lawn without a Bible in your hands announced what you are. If you wanted to stay private, you would have stayed home. Stop fretting over it.*

The trouble is, I'm great at fretting and much, much worse at letting go of anything.

"You were amazing," Evaline told me while we ate some hot chili at a little diner afterward. "You really stepped up, Rose. We needed that today. I'm proud of you."

I chuckled. "I wasn't really trying to lead. I was just trying to do something good."

Evaline laughed. "I'm fairly certain that's what real leaders do."

Robin, sitting next to me in the booth, swept a stray lock of hair over my shoulder. "You are not afraid to speak, my Rose; nor do you shirk from the work. You are lucky to live in a remarkably welcoming time for the witch. It is good and right that you are fighting to keep it so."

"Thanks," I said, still fretting. "I was just thinking how I'm kind of lousy with the fourth power of the Sphinx. The first three I've got nailed. 'To know.' Yes, I know stuff. Not as much as Grace, but I am still pretty knowledgeable. 'To will.' When I put my mind to something it gets done. 'To dare.' Check. I think we all have that one. Performing witchcraft in the daylight on government property is pretty damned daring of us." They nodded, laughing and more than a little impressed at their own boldness. "But I don't seem to be very good at 'To keep silent.' I always have to say the thing I'm thinking."

Evaline shrugged. "Sometimes." She laughed. "Okay, a lot of the time. You are a very verbal person, Rose. But I know that you can keep secrets."

"Discretion is often the better part of valor," Robin said. "But that implies knowing when it is wisest to be silent. The other half of that wisdom is knowing when it is imperative to speak."

I nodded. I was starting to feel self-conscious. Yes, I'm remarkable, and I totally did the right thing today. Let's talk about this chili now, or the NFL, or anything other than me and the fact that I'm a known witch who's going to show up on the evening news.

"So, Robin, you're still at Evaline's for a few days, yes?" I asked. Smooth transition. I'm good at those.

He reached his hand across the table to Evie. "Just tonight, actually. We have something special planned. Would you like to join us?"

Uh. Huh?

I looked across the table to Evaline and then back at Robin. Did I just get invited to a ménage a trois? The shock must have been plain on my face. They both laughed at me.

"We're doing some magic, hon," Evie said. "Robin and I have been talking about my connection to the wolf. We're going to do a shapeshifter ritual to protect the pack, the coven."

My hairs were standing on end again. "That sounds awesome," I said. "But I don't have any wolfy connections. I'm not sure what I could do."

"You could lend energy," Robin said. "You may not have wolf as a totem, but you are part of the pack."

We had all known that Evaline had wolf totem. Wolf was a potent personal symbol for her. We all had totem animals that bespoke some aspect of our nature. Totems plants, too, if we were honest. Lilly and I had names that connected us with the energies of two such plants.

Evaline's wolf connection went further than that, though. Wolf was a part of her spirit. When we did work on the astral plane, meditative work that took our spirits outside of our bodies, we could all see the wolf-woman that was Evie.

She couldn't wear silver close to her skin, either. We had given her a silver ring when she joined the coven, but the band ate through her skin. It didn't burn her quickly like you see in movies, but it didn't sit comfortably on her, either. Her skin peeled and flaked around it. I had to tell her she could carry it in a pouch or wear it on a chain outside of her shirt, if she wanted. Eventually, we bought her a white gold ring instead.

Our coven had never done shapeshifting magic. I was interested, but it also felt intrusive. I'd like us all to do it. Barring that, maybe it was best if I sat it out.

"I think I'll lend energy from home tonight, if that's okay," I said. "I think I need a little introversion time after today's festivities."

"That's fair," Evaline said. "I'm going to let the others know, too. You can fly out to join us. We plan on starting at midnight."

By midnight, I planned on being asleep. The solitary drive back to my house in West Nowhere, Indiana made me sleepier than I thought possible. I stumbled in, giving Grace a quick hug and telling her about Evaline's working. Her energy felt brighter than it had in days, and I had the impression that she wanted to hang out and visit. We hadn't done that in several days. I'd been busy, and she'd been isolating herself. But the weight of my need for sleep was pressing in on me, and I apologized before heading to bed. She and Lilly could hang out tonight. Maybe we could spend some time together tomorrow. Her shoulders drooped just a little as she hugged me good night.

I stripped off my clothes, leaving them in a puddle on my bedroom floor. Tomorrow I would be tidy. I lit the white novena candle that sat on my dresser. The beads of what looked like a sparkling bracelet clinked on the glass candle holder. It wasn't actually a bracelet. We called it a candle ladder. It was a talisman, a beaded version of the protection cords we made with Bea. This one was made to represent the coven, each of us contributing a special bead or charm to the others' ladders. We used them to do spells to benefit the coven. Or, like tonight, we could use them to link to the others in astral magic.

My jar of flying ointment stayed in the drawer next to my bed. I made an awesome salve that wouldn't kill you like the old-fashioned blends could, the ones featuring belladonna, hemlock, and aconite. I wasn't above using some yummy hallucinogens in my magic, but accidental poisoning wasn't high on my to-do list. Some of the classic flying potions needed a practiced hand to formulate. Sadly, that lore didn't get passed down to me, and I don't want to use trial and error on my coven sisters to figure out which blend would be both efficacious and non-fatal.

I made a mental note to ask Robin's advice about using the old poisons in magic. He should know. In the meantime, I would use my modern blend, assured that I wouldn't wake up dead from my twilight sleep.

The green grease smeared easily onto the soles of my feet, the backs of my knees, into my armpits. My blend smelled like Italian food. It was the Dittany of Crete. It's basically an oregano. I'd wash the sheets tomorrow. Maybe order a pizza, too.

I clicked my mp3 player on and popped the earbuds into my ears. It was well before midnight, but I reminded myself that time is a human construct that had no bearing on the astral plane.

I'd said this so many times to myself and my sisters that it sounded sing-songy and child-like in my head, like kids giving a pat response to a teacher's oft-repeated question.

Right. So, time isn't really a thing. At least, it's not a thing on certain levels of reality. Quantum physicists can explain it better than I can. It's enough for me to have experienced, several times, that time doesn't really matter for magic. All I needed to know was that I could go right now to the time and place where Robin and Evaline were doing their magic. And that's exactly where I was going.

I drifted on the waves of the ambient trance music piping into my brain. I breathed deeply and walked myself through the same relaxation and centering exercise through which Grace led the coven at Robin's summoning. I breathed my energy in and up, out and down. I let myself expand and float above my body. I saw myself floating on a little round raft in a foggy sea. The bobbing of the waves was peaceful, and I settled into the rhythm. I was in no rush. I closed my eyes, the astral ones, given that my physical eyes had been shut since I first lay down. I felt the rocking of the waves, felt myself a part of them. I stretched my energetic body, feeling my neck long and graceful. I opened my eyes and looked down into the water, my snow white wings folded around my buoyant body.

"Flying out" is the old witchcraft term for what the New Agers call astral projection. Witches have traditionally done it one of two ways. The first is on a riding pole, like a broom or a forked stang or a staff. This is often the first way that we learn to fly. The pole is symbolic of the world tree whose branches support the heavens and whose roots are in the Underworld. With the riding pole, you can go up, down, or anywhere in between.

The other way witches "fly out" is by shapeshifting. Old George Pickingill, an infamous Welsh cunning man of the late 1800's, had a coven that was known to locals to take the shape of rabbits. Some covens roam the night as goats. Some as wolves. Our coven has only one wolf. We're a bit of a motley crew. Myself, I like to fly as a swan.

Shapeshifting for us didn't mean that our physical bodies became animals. I believe that is possible, in theory. I think. Or maybe it doesn't actually work that way, but rather the shapeshifter is able to astral project so forcefully that their spirit manifests in a very tangible way. I felt certain *that* was possible. After all, our coven had manifested Robin. He was definitely *here*. If we could do that, it had to be possible to make your own living spirit walk and talk and touch, too.

Of course, then the question becomes: *What happens with your physical body while your spirit is busy being all physical somewhere else?* It's an excellent question that I didn't have a good answer to. For now, let's just say that it sleeps and breathes and needs to be protected while the spirit is out to play. I knew, without really thinking about it, that my body was doing that even now.

This wasn't the time to focus on my body, though. Too much thought in that direction would find me right back in it. I was out, and I looked up into the gloaming sky. This place is between places, between times. It is neither dark nor day. Neither dawn nor dusk. Or maybe it is both.

I could feel which way I needed to go to find Evaline and Robin. I knew where my coven met in this betwixt and between. I stretched my long neck toward the heavens, my breast raised above the water. I beat my wings against the air, water rippling below me. Two solid beats and I was up and above the sea. Several more and I was soaring into the gray-gold sky.

I pointed myself toward the mountain. I could see it in the distance. Flap. Glide. Repeat.

The air was cold and damp. You wouldn't think those details would exist in the astral, but it's astonishing what you can sense when you're not in your body. I could feel more than the physical sensations that a body feels. More than the emotions. I had senses for which I had no words. I could feel the height of my flight. I could feel all the space between me and the ground, like a spongy cushion below me. I could hear the starlight above me. I could smell the directions.

The mountain loomed into view as I drew closer. I saw the clearing where the Sabbat bonfire would be lit. It was not the Sabbat, not the holy night when scores of witches came to this same place to frolic. No bonfire glowed in the glen. I circled the mountain and found our private place, our grove. It was a special place, warded and separate from the bonfire field. Other witches had other places, but this one was our coven's grove. It was open only to us, invisible to all but those bound to our covenant by blood.

Robin was there. He stood naked and glorious, ringed by torches, their flames leaping and laughing under the canopy of trees. He looked different here. More familiar. I had seen him here a hundred times or more. Ruddy-skinned and barrel-chested. And the horns. Oh my giddy aunt, those horns! Four great curling goat horns. His chin made the fifth point of the classic inverted pentagram. If I had knees as a swan, I think they would have buckled.

I said, or rather, I *thought*, "Weren't you doing a wolf thing?"

Evaline came out of the line of trees. She looked like Evaline, the human version; but she *felt* wilder. Her eyes definitely looked like something other than human Evie. They were yellow, for one thing. She walked around the circle, her eyes on Robin as she moved. He matched her, giving me a wink before he turned his full attention on her. They walked the circle. No, they stalked the circle. Prowled. Loped. The flicker of the torches cast light and shadow over them. I didn't notice when they stopped looking human-ish and started looking entirely like wolves. She was dark gray with white and black markings. He was solid black.

I looked around and saw three other shapes in the clearing. There was a little owl, the size of a saw whet, looking vulnerable and surprised with her too-big eyes. That was Grace. Lilly was the jaguar glaring out from the shadows. Pearl must be the goat this time. She enjoyed experimenting with different shapes. Last time, she came as a dragon. Yes, you can do that.

We didn't look the same, inside or out. We didn't feel the same. We didn't do the same work, have the same taste in clothes.

115

We didn't find the same men – or women – attractive, with the notable exception of Robin. We definitely didn't like the same music. But these people were my dearest friends, my family. My chosen family. I would die for them. I would probably rob a bank for them. I would definitely trade my privacy for their anonymity. I would defend them to my last bloody breath, if the situation called for it. And let's be honest, it might. This was my pack.

The wolves prowled the circle, starting on the outer edges and winding their way to the middle. I could feel them marking the boundaries of the space. They were laying down a scent, a sensation, a prickling on the back of the neck as a warning to the world not to harm us.

I don't remember the owl, the jaguar, the goat, or myself moving to the four directions, but when the wolves stalked into the center point of the compass and looked at us in turn, I saw that we were at our stations. Grace, the night bird, was in the north, which is elemental air for us. Lilly, the jaguar, was in the east. Fire. Pearl, the goat, was in the south. Earth. I was the water bird in the west. Water.

The wolves lifted their heads and howled, low at first. We joined them in sounding a call. Again, the howling, louder this time. A third and final howl, joined by bleats and hoots, growls and my own trumpeting honk.

We may have looked and sounded odd, but the message was clear. We will fight for each other by tooth, beak, talon, hoof, horn, and claw.

Chapter 16

Maybe it's possessive of me, but I was over the moon when Robin decided to come back to my house. I'd missed him, more than it had occurred to me that I could.

Evaline didn't tell me about their escapades, and I didn't ask. She wasn't a kisser and teller, and I am not the sort to ask. Pearl asked.

"Did you do it?" Sometimes Pearl is a fifteen-year-old boy.

Evaline didn't blush. I love that about her. She might not talk about the details of her sex life, but she wasn't prudish or shy about having one. "Oh, yeah," she said with a grin. But that was all she said.

Pearl waited for more, and then lost patience. "Was it totally hot? I mean, it was like the best sex ever for me."

Evie's eyebrows popped up once as if nodding with the rest of her head. "Yeah, it sure was."

Pearl waited for more explication. None came. "Is it weird that I want details?"

Evie hit her with a throw pillow from my couch. "A little, you perv."

I decided to take the conversation to a theoretical place. "So, I have an idea," I said, turning their attention my way. "In the old trial records, witches often admit to having sex with their familiar spirits and with the devil himself."

"It's hard to tell what's true and what was said only because of torture in those records," Evaline said.

Grace and Lilly came out of Lilly's room where they'd been painting. "True," Grace said, sitting on the couch next to me. "But

117

we know that some of it is accurate. We have uncovered too many real things that were referenced in the records. I mean, Robin Artisson's name is first mentioned in Dame Alice's trial. And we know he's real."

"And we can assume," I said, "that the part about them having sex is also true. I mean, we all had a sexual awakening with the spirit of Robin long before he was here with us. And now that he's here, we might be able to assume that it will happen in the physical realm, too. It's already happened with three of us, for sure."

I looked at Grace and Lilly, the only two that hadn't confirmed sexy time with Robin yet. I couldn't read either of them, but I knew that Lilly hadn't had the opportunity.

Grace shrugged, "Maybe. We'll see."

"It just feels weird," Pearl said, "that we're all having sex with the same guy. But it also feels weird to me because I just don't care, and I feel like I'm supposed to care."

The guy himself said, "Witches are transgressive, my dear." So much for the nap he was taking. I guess the five of us talking about sex had his ears burning. "Sex is yet another way to thumb your nose at the imposed morals and dogma of a Puritanical culture."

"Is that all it is, then?" I asked, my crest having visibly fallen. "Witches have sex with spirits just to be deviant. Like reading the Lord's Prayer backwards at midnight at the crossroads? It's just another way to flip the bird to Christians?" I didn't mind doing things that were counter-culture, but I saw no value in being oppositional just for the sake of opposition.

Robin sat in the floor in the middle of us. "No, not necessarily. It isn't just a 'fuck you' to the moral majority. But that is all they can see in it. All they are able to see is the aberration. Women are thought to be detached from their sexual nature. Holy virgins. Or else they are the source of all lust, which is seen as dirty, defiling, and base. Women who revel in sex are whores, the *Moral Ones* say. Whores and witches, enchanting men with sex. Inflaming them with desire. Sometimes punishing them by toppling the towers of their libido with impotence."

Pearl said, "There's still slut-shaming today, but there's also feminism and empowerment. There's Planned Parenthood in every county, and sex toy parties are way more popular than Avon and Tupperware."

"Yes," Robin said. "And the concept of polyamory, of loving more than one person, exists more openly now than it has in millennia. But it is still seen as aberrant, deviant, scandalous, and immoral by most people – even people who don't see themselves as conservative."

"So, is that what this coven is?" I asked. "A poly family?"

Robin considered my question. He looked at each of us. "You all love each other," he said. "Some of you have romantic affections. Some of you are more filial. All of you have had sex with each other." He winked. "I know. I saw it." Grace and I held hands and smooshed our shoulders together. Robin continued, "By some definitions, you are all in a poly relationship."

Pearl's eyebrows went up and the corners of her mouth pulled down. "Huh," she said. "I really hadn't thought of it like that."

"And what about your place in this poly family, Robin?" Lilly asked, grinning like she already knew the answer.

"I am the magister of the coven," he said. "I am at the center. The devil at the crossroads."

It was my turn to be blunt. "And is having a sexual relationship with all of us part of that job?"

"My relationship with each of you doesn't actually have to be sexual," he said. "But if it is, it is. What it must be is *intimate*." He looked at us each in turn, starting with Evaline. "You must each know that are my witch, my lover, my daughter, my sister." He paused, ending with me. "My wife."

I flushed.

Lilly asked, "Are we all of those things."

Robin chose his words carefully. "You are all at least one of those things, yes."

Pearl asked, with a lilt in her voice, "So, maybe I'm a lover and a daughter?"

"Sounds taboo, doesn't it?" Robin winked at her. "Incest is certainly a transgressive concept, and not one that needs to be so literal in its translation to be powerful. After all, I am not your earthly father, nor a physical brother. We share little more in the way of genetics than you share with any stranger on the other side of the globe."

"Ooh. You can be my very own dirty daddy," Pearl giggled. "But not so icky. I like it."

He wagged his eyebrows at her, and Pearl giggled again.

I wasn't sure I could think about them playing in that way. I didn't get the appeal. Not at all. In fact, it sort of squicked me out. I pushed it aside, knowing there isn't any real harm in the fantasy of incest play, as long as nobody's getting hurt in the process. But … yeah. Count me out.

"So," I brought the topic back around to our connections, "we each have a special relationship with you, regardless of whether or not we have sex with you."

"That is correct," he said. "Rather, I should say that I need to have a special relationship with each of you. You are all witches, of course. More specifically, you are all *my* witches. You are under my protection and my tutelage. You are descended, whether you realize it or not, from other witches with whom I have danced in the woods on long ago midnights."

I raised my eyebrows. "Anyone we would have heard of?"

"No, not for the most part," Robin said. "Most of them kept their anonymity … and their lives."

"Most?" asked Evaline. "But not all."

"No, not all," Robin said. He looked down at his hands for a moment. When he spoke again, he looked directly at Evie. "You are descended from Petronilla de Meath. She was the servant of

Dame Alice Kettle. Petronilla was the first to be burned at the stake for heresy in Ireland. Poor Pet."

Evaline's eyes turned hard. She was angry at the long-dead men who had tortured and killed Petronilla.

"And you, Rose," he looked at me, and there was something like longing or loneliness in the look. "You are the many-times great-granddaughter of Alice herself."

My breath caught in my throat.

"Alice had a son and two daughters, all of whom escaped the torturous death encountered by both Alice and her maid. You," he said looking into my eyes, "are descended from Rose Outlaw."

A shiver ran through my spine, that shiver that tells me when I've heard something both true and significant.

"Wait," I said. "I thought Alice escaped and fled to England. She never shows up in the records again. It was presumed she escaped."

He shook his head. "Sadly, that is false. Ledrede, the bishop who condemned her, caught her on the road before she reached safety. He hurt her in ways you should never know before finally killing her."

My stomach was churning. This was my ancestor. My I-don't-even-know-how-many-times great grandmother. In an instant, this woman I had only read about became family to me. She became like a mother whose story I knew very well. I could see her frightened face in the firelight of the deranged bishop's pyre. He burned her, after torturing her. He threatened her daughter's life, and not only her life. I wept for Alice. And I wept for Rose, alone in the world after her mother had been ripped from her. An outlaw indeed.

"Rose was not alone," Robin said, evidently knowing my thoughts. He looked at me with deep tenderness. "I was able to come to her, as I am here with you now. She called me in the forest, as her mother had taught her. I never left her."

I looked into his eyes, fat tear drops clinging to my eyelashes and running down my cheeks. "And I am your great-great-great granddaughter?"

"More great than that," he said, laughing just a little at his own joke and wiping my tears with his sleeve. "It is actually what made my coming to you possible. It is why I am the familiar for this coven. I am *your* familiar. You inherited me."

I blinked. "Me and Evie, you mean?"

"No, Rose," he said. "Just you."

The others were suddenly very still. Pearl snorted. "Always so special."

My shoulders sagged. I didn't like being singled out from the rest of the coven. Even when it was something good, I still felt bad.

"You are all special to me," Robin reassured them, looking at each in turn again. "And I need a special relationship with each of you, just as I said. But without Rose, I wouldn't have been able to come to you. It is my blood in her veins, and Rose Outlaw's blood, that allows me to be here."

We all sat in silence, listening to the wind whistling outside the door. A storm was coming.

Chapter 17

"Grace is having another emotional drop, it seems," Robin came to the basement library to tell Lilly and me. "I think she needs some time and attention. If it's okay with you ladies, I'm going to spend an hour or so with her. I believe a proper snuggle is in order."

As far as I was concerned, Robin could do almost anything he wanted, as long as he said it in that yummy accent. "A proper snuggle" sounded warm and delicious. I had to assume he meant sex, of course, given the recent relationship talk we all had. Although he had mentioned that sex wasn't required with all of us. Just intimacy.

"Give her hugs for me," I said.

Lilly frowned and nodded her concern at him. He winked and turned away, leaving us both a bit giggly. That man and his winks!

Lilly was frowning again when I turned my attention back to her. "Grace isn't holding up very well, is she?"

I shrugged and then shook my head. "Not really. I've seen her depressed before. Anxious. But, yeah, this is different. She refuses to talk about the stuff with Sewall or the murders. That damned registry has been off the table as a point of discussion for weeks, regardless of how it impacts us all."

Lilly nodded, the frown still creasing her forehead. "I hope she feels better after all this is over."

"Me, too," I said. "But I'm worried about her, and it's more than just this recent stuff."

"What else?" Lilly asked.

I thought about my response for a moment. I didn't want to gossip about Grace, but I also needed to talk through her behavior with someone. Lilly had been living in the house with us long enough to have noticed a few things, and I was hoping she could help me gain some perspective or reclaim a little patience. "She hasn't been herself for a few months, Lilly. She isn't the Grace I met six years ago. She isn't interested in any of the things that brought us together as friends. Not even witchcraft is all that compelling to her anymore, and I would have sworn it was her passion in those early years."

Lilly nodded. "I've noticed that. She never does card readings with us anymore, and she only talks about magic in a theoretical way. She usually turns down all her chances to do magic with the coven."

"Right," I agreed, grateful that I wasn't the only one who saw the changes. I'd tried mentioning it to Evaline, but she'd suggested that Grace was just tired and would pull out of it. "I've pleaded with her a few times to do a reading for me or work on the Ouija board with me, but she gets exhausted so easily now, and she gets moody, too. She's sullen and snappish with me, and it's not just about magic."

Lilly sighed. "Yeah, I've noticed that, too. She's patient with almost everyone else, but she gets mad at you really fast."

"I'm not the easiest person to get along with," I admitted, "and I'm probably a pain to live with. Grace tells me I nag her all the time."

"A little, yeah," Lilly agreed. "But I wouldn't say it's all the time."

"There are some reminders I've been giving Grace since we moved in together," I said. "I'm always having to remind her to rinse her hair out of the tub, wipe drops of pee and period blood off the toilet seat, and clean her cat's litter box."

Lilly made a disgusted face. "Ew."

"I know," I said. "Six years of some really gross habits. And I don't think I am being unreasonable by asking her to take care of those things."

"Not at all," Lilly said. "It's basic courtesy. You don't leave your freakin' menstrual blood on the toilet seat. That's just nasty."

"Right?" I sighed. "But when I remind her, she acts like I'm her mom and she's a teenager. Like I'm being so demanding."

I chewed on the side of my mouth for a minute and digested my thoughts. Grace and I were having trouble. I'd been worried about our relationship, such as it was, for a while. We didn't have much sexual chemistry to begin with, although there had been some initial sparks. When we first got to know each other, we used to get drunk and make out like horny teenagers. We embarrassed one of our younger witch-friends at a solstice celebration with our pawing and kissing and giggling. The poor girl was just starting to figure out that she was a lesbian, and there we were broadcasting the sexy-lezzie vibe.

We cooled off right after that incident, though. Froze up, actually. When we did try to have sex, we were both awkward and uncomfortable, though for different reasons. I liked that Grace was responsive to my touch. She always came. Multiple times, actually. But she rarely had those big orgasms that signal the end of the session. And I never got off. Well, once. Okay twice. I had two orgasms with Grace in our six years of living together.

Between lack of staying power and poor body awareness, Grace was just never able to figure out how to get me there. She tried using her hand and got a cramp in her forearm. Tried oral, and got a cramp in her neck. We tried strap-ons, and that was a bust. When she'd find an angle or rhythm that really worked, she couldn't hold it for more than about five strokes. We even tried a couple of variations on scissoring, but she would always get so turned on once I started to climax that she would beat me to the finish line, leaving both of us unwilling and unable to try again.

Eventually, I gave up. I'm not an easy lover, and I had started to think that maybe I just wasn't built for sex with women.

We were both open to other lovers, and we went on dates from time to time. I liked to think that we were both getting our needs met from them, and our relationship was strong enough to endure "lesbian bed death."

I was just considering voicing some of this to Lilly when Robin came back into her room.

"That was fast," I said.

He nodded. "She cried herself to sleep in my arms."

Lilly and I both frowned. Poor Grace. She was miserable, and I felt helpless. "Did she say anything about what's wrong?"

He shook his head. "I think she is having a fit of melancholy that she can't shake. It could be demon possession. Or ghost sickness."

I looked up at him, surprise covering my face. "Really?"

He nodded, a concerned frown knitting his brows together, and then he laughed. "No, not really. It's melancholy … or, um … depression."

"Ah," I said. "Well, we knew that much already. What do we do to help her?"

He drew his lips between his teeth, considering the options. "We help her banish the demon."

"I get that you're using a metaphor," I said, "but given her response to our current demon situation, the metaphor is almost literal. The only trouble is that she was doing poorly before this whack-job coven started their demon evocation. Banishing that demon should help, but I fear there is another *demon* waiting just around the corner for Grace."

"Maybe so," he said. "We have to take this one piece at a time. Don't borrow trouble. Fearing for the future won't make it any brighter, but it can certainly make today darker."

Truth. Anxiety sucks.

"And you can't change the past," Lilly added.

I nodded, but Robin held a finger aloft. "Ah, but you can," he said. "At least, you can alter portions of it. There are several techniques you can use to rewrite the past. Reality is, after all, largely what you believe it to be. You can rewrite your own past by choosing to believe that events happened in a certain way. People do this all the time."

"I see," Lilly said. "Like a friend I had in college who always exaggerated her stories. Everything was larger than life when she retold a story. If someone was curt with her, she believed they were unimaginably rude. If a guy liked her, she believed he was pining away for her. I remember this one time that she had a little car accident. She slid off the road in snow and came to a stop in some bushes near a three foot deep ditch. She told everyone that she almost died." Lilly snorted. "The funny thing is that she seemed to believe that she had really come close to dying. Even if her car had gone into the ditch, she wouldn't have been anything more than a little sore from getting jostled. But she was a hot mess for the whole rest of the winter. She wouldn't drive if there was even the threat of flurries."

Robin smiled. "Yes, this young woman was certainly skilled at rewriting her past. The series of events that she created for herself were as strong as any memory and certainly impacted her life and her decisions in the same way. I wonder how often she used this ability for self-improvement and optimism."

Lilly shrugged. "Don't know. She did do it some, but mainly she seemed to exaggerate things so that she came off sympathetic. She seemed to enjoy being the damsel in distress."

"I know a witch in Cincinnati who is a therapist," I interjected. "She and I had a fascinating talk last summer about neuro-linguistic programming. Some of what you're saying reminds me of that."

"Perhaps," Robin conceded. "I would have to do some study to say with certainty, but I can tell you one thing without doubt. The word is a powerful creation tool. There is a reason the Abrahamic faiths believe their God *spoke* the universe into being. What we say about ourselves, our environments, and our experiences shapes our lives. The idea of a *spell* is based on the power of the word to create change."

I thought for a moment. "That is true, and it is a powerful concept. But we were talking about Grace. We can't change her past with our words, can we?"

Robin was silent and still for a few moments. "I'm not sure. There are too many situations in flux right now, and it may well be that Grace needs to ride out the uncomfortable feelings she is having."

Lilly and I both looked down at the pattern in the fake Persian rug. I had hoped maybe we could help Grace out with a little metaphysical aid.

"But there is another," Robin began, "whom I am certain we can help."

Our eyes snapped back to him. "Who?" I asked.

Robin looked sad and strained. "Dame Alice Kettle."

"What?" Lilly and I asked in unison.

"She died alone and in terrible agony," he said, his voice strained. "The man who tortured and killed her took great care in abusing my poor Alice. At that time, we didn't know about dwale. This was the beginning of those terrible trials. And by the time I learned, Alice had no coven to bring the dwale to her."

I interrupted. "*Dwale*? I'm sorry, Robin, but I don't know what that is."

"Dwale is succor and release for a witch in direst need," he said. "Dwale is deadly nightshade, that witches' berry."

"You mean belladonna?" I asked.

He nodded, and his eyes were grim. "Indeed. During the hottest years of the Burning, a witch could be assured that someone would bring her this potent plant ally before the fires were lit beneath her or she was put to the machines designed to end her life."

"I've never used belladonna," I admitted. I remembered that I'd intended to ask him about belladonna and the other flying herbs. Looks like a bit of education on the poison path had found me. "I know a little about it but nothing from practical experience."

Robin nodded. "She is not an herb to meddle with, that *pretty lady*. She commands respect and attention. The person who fails to give her close attention can pay a fatal price."

Lilly wasn't an herbalist, and she didn't know as much about deadly nightshade as even I did. She asked, "If dwale is such a poisonous plant, why call it *pretty lady*? Why not call it something scary? I know they do that with other herbs."

"Well, *deadly nightshade* isn't a name that invites confidence," Robin began. "Nor is *dwale*, really. In the old language, it means things like error and heresy. The Italians called it belladonna because ladies would squeeze small drops of the juice into their eyes to make their pupils large. It was considered very feminine and beautiful."

"Belladonna extract was still used to dilate pupils at optometrists' offices before an eye exam until just a few years ago," I added. "We've both had belladonna in our own eyes at least once or twice. They use some sort of synthetic now, though."

"It was used in childbirth, when the pain was unbearable for the mother," Robin said. "But most importantly, it was used in flying salve."

"Is that how it was used to bring relief to a burning witch, then?" I asked. "I've been curious about using the traditional herbs in that way."

"Yes," he said. "With opium and hemlock, belladonna produces a powerful drink that is responsible for the twilight sleep. The sensation is much like flying out to the Sabbat, with only negligible differences. Surgeons once used dwale for operations, and midwives used it during difficult births. Those same midwives often used it within their covens to fly to the Sabbat, or, as we will do, to ease the terrible passing of a sister."

My heart fluttered. I couldn't tell if I was terrified or excited. Both, probably. "Are we going to make dwale and drink it?"

Robin thought for a moment. "We could," he said. "How much opium do you have in your herb supply?"

I laughed right out loud. "None," I said, still laughing, though I knew he hadn't meant to be funny. "Opium is a controlled substance. Doctors only give you morphine, which is made from opium," I explained, "if you are in serious pain. And heroin, a drug made from those poppy seeds, is flat-out illegal."

Robin looked confused and concerned. "There are herbs you are not permitted to grow or use in your own home medicines?" He sounded incredulous.

"Don't get me started," I said.

Lilly was chuckling. She knew I wasn't much of a pot smoker, but I had championed its use for sufferers of chronic pain, anxiety, and other ailments. I was looking forward to the day when Indiana adopted a medical marijuana policy. I wasn't holding my breath, though. That day could be a long way off.

Robin blinked several times, trying to sort that news into a useful category. "Well," he stammered, "we don't …. It's possible to take dwale to her without ingesting it ourselves. I hesitate to ask if you have any deadly nightshade."

"You know," I answered brightly, "as it just so happens, I do."

Robin looked very confused now. "How is that possible? You don't have poppy seeds, but you do have deadly nightshade."

I shrugged. "Beats me. I'm allowed to grow it, so I have it. I actually have quite a nice little poison garden. I use the plants energetically in things like poppets and spell bags."

He nodded. "I'd like to see what other herbs you have available. Belladonna by itself can cause very unpleasant visions. It was never used by itself. A quick look in your pantry will give us some options, if we do choose to ingest a bit of the dwale to take to Alice."

I showed him to my herb cabinet. He was impressed. It was actually an old china cabinet that I'd purchased secondhand and filled with glass canning jars which were, in turn, filled with herbs. He chose a few items while I diligently took notes in my journal.

Lilly, it seems, was preparing the temple room for our ritual. We returned to lit candles and Lilly in her black robes.

Chapter 18

Robin slipped the extra black robe over his head. I was feeling grateful that I had made myself a new one and was able to loan him my old robe. It would have been such a tragedy to be nude with him. Ha.

While Robin prepared the dwale, Lilly and I made an incense featuring vervain, juniper berries, mugwort, and amber oil. It was missing something. I always liked to blend incense using the acronym FLOWR, which reminded me to include at least one flower, leaf, oil, wood, and resin in the mix. Berries or fruit could replace the blossom, and we had juniper. Check. Both vervain and mugwort counted as leaves. Check. Amber oil. Check. We still needed a wood and a resin. I chose myrrh tears and white willow, both of which are used medicinally as pain relievers. They should lend that soothing, anesthetic energy to the incense, as well.

Lilly had lit the charcoal disk along with the candles, so it was glowing and ready for incense. I handed her the little jar, and she pinched some of the mixture onto the waiting coal. Thick curls of smoke wafted into the air, and we all took a deep breath of the fumes.

"This is a major working," I said. "Let's take a moment to cleanse the temple of residual energies before we begin."

Robin and Lilly both nodded and moved to the edges of the space, giving me room to circumambulate. I grabbed the broom, sweeping the floor, the ceiling, and the space in between as I circled the room three times. "Besom sweep and besom clean – above, below, and in between. Let nothing harmful here be found as we tread the witches' round." I bowed to the stang, the witch's pitchfork, in its patio umbrella stand in the center of the room before laying the broom at the southern edge of the room.

Lilly picked up the incense burner, swinging it on its chains in large circles in front of her as she walked. "Smoke and fume, now as you burn, cause all harm from us to turn. Let nothing harmful here be found as we tread the witches' round." She bowed to the center before setting the hot brass thurible on a ceramic tile in the northern part of the room.

I mixed salt into a chalice of water. "Water and salt, brine of the sea, wash this circle clean and free. Let nothing harmful here be found as we tread the witches' round." I bowed to the center, and placed the cup in the west.

Lilly walked with the red candle from the east. "Fire that burns and light that glows, send all harm away from us. Let nothing harmful here be found as we tread the witches' round." She bowed to the center and returned the candle to its spot on the floor.

We all breathed deeply again. As much as this short preparatory ritual was useful in cleansing and warding a space before ritual, it was equally useful in centering our attention on the work at hand.

Robin stepped to the center of the compass and lifted the stang out of its holder. It seemed so natural, him holding our three-pronged staff. This stang represented the World Tree on which Odin hung to find wisdom and magic, the place of initiation, of access to all the worlds and realms of creation. It would look like an old wooden hayfork to the uninitiated. Well, it would look like a hayfork upon which some crazy witch had hung a goat skull with a candle between its horns.

I smiled when I remembered that such a tool was out of the norm for the common person. In fact, I bet our stang would scare the bejeezus out of most folks. I've been practicing witchcraft so long that a skull on a forked stick doesn't seem out of the ordinary to me anymore.

I get it, though. To the average Jill, this might as well be the pitchfork of the devil himself. She would see it as the torture device

Old Nick would use to skewer sinners and torment saints. This was not a tool we'd be taking to the next protest on the courthouse lawn.

This strange staff, this pitchfork, was more than just the riding pole of the witch, more than even the World Tree it represented. It was a simple embodiment of the Witch Father himself. In the center of our circle, this compass where the crossroads meet, the horns of the stang bespoke the horns of the God. They were the horns of the sabbatic goat, the antlers of the Lord of the Forest. They reminded us that we are primal, earthy beings with a spiritual nature. The candle flame was the cunning fire. The three prongs showed us the left- and right-hand paths and the middle path of the witch. Neither dark nor light, but grey. The herb that heals can also kill. It is for the practitioner to know, to will, and to dare its use.

Robin leaned on the stang and started his walk around the circle. The stang struck the floor with a loud thud each time he stepped forward, and then he dragged his back foot behind. He was literally tracing the circle using what I recognized as the "lame step" though I had never seen anyone use it this way.

Forge Gods are almost universally crippled or lamed in some way. Blame it on heavy metal poisoning drawing up the hamstrings of the Iron Age blacksmith. Or blame it on the villagers injuring the blacksmith to keep him in town. Or blame it on his fall from Olympus (or Heaven, depending on the mythology you like best). Whatever the reason, the blacksmith often walked with an uneven step, and so did the Gods who represented him. The Witch Father is epitomized by the forge and the smith. Tubal Cain. Lucifer. Shamash. Robin was walking in the Red God's footsteps.

I fell to my knees in front of the anvil and took up the hammer. I struck the hammer to the anvil and cried out, "Tubal Cain!" I struck again. "Tubal Cain!" And a third time. "Tubal Cain!"

His crooked path finished, Robin stepped to the center, his amber eyes glowing with a deep fire, the stang still in his hands. The man with the horns at the crossroads. I trembled in fear and delight.

He put the stang back in its holder and held a hand out to each of us. Lilly and I came to him, linking hands with him and each other.

"We stand between that which has been and that which will be," he began. "We stand in the center of the eternal now, and we hear a fallen sister calling for aid. Do you know what we must do?"

"Yes," Lilly and I both replied.

"Is it your will to do this thing?" he asked.

"Yes," we replied.

"And do you dare to do so?"

"Yes."

"Then I place an oath upon us all," he said, "that this work should be kept secret and not spoken of to anyone outside this coven."

He picked up the flask of fresh dwale and held it between us. Lilly and I continued holding each other's hands. We might be daring enough to drink poison to help Dame Alice, but we were still understandably scared.

Robin took a slug from the bottle and handed it to Lilly. She took a drink, tasted her lips, and frowned. It wasn't a look of displeasure. Rather, it was one of discernment. Analysis. I'd seen her make the same face while trying to detect what spice had been used in a chicken dish – and trying to decide if she liked it.

Lilly passed the bottle to me, and I took my drink. The berry flavor was cloyingly sweet, and the brew was threaded with a bitter herbal taste that I recognized as wormwood. There was something rooty in the mix, too, but I couldn't place it.

I set the flask back at the base of the stang and looked back to Robin for direction. He had already told us that we'd have dry mouth from the elixir, and there were water bottles nearby. He'd also told us that we'd be hallucinating for several hours and not to be worried about that. Nor should we panic if we got sick. We took precautions, and now we had a little time before the twilight sleep began.

The room was warm to me, and I could feel the heat baking my cheeks. I pulled my robe over my head and laid it aside. Lilly did the same, her dark hair spilling over her enormous breasts.

Robin laid on his side and gestured for us to lie down as well. I closed my eyes and listened to his voice as he said, "We bring the dwale to Dame Alice Kyteler. Alice, we come to you across the years. Your coven is here. Dwale has found you."

Through the darkness of my own eyelids, I felt myself walking in a midnight forest. A campfire glowed ahead, and I picked my way through the underbrush as silently as I could manage. Rustling leaves and snapping twigs to my right and left told me that Lilly and Robin were with me.

The woman was beautiful in the firelight, her coppery hair falling like a blaze around her shoulders and down her back. Her hands were bound to a fallen log, jutting her exposed breasts toward the priest who leered at her, knife in hand. He had pulled or hacked her cloths from her body and thrown them in the fire. Alice looked defiantly at him, giving her hair a shake. It shimmered like copper flame.

When she spoke, I heard the odd French-Irish accent that I supposed was what the historians meant by calling her "Hiberno-Norman." I heard the accent, but I also heard words that sounded like modern English. "You are a coward, Priest," she laughed. "A coward and a fool."

"You are no one to speak of cowardice, Witch," he spat back at her. "I caught you fleeing the Lord's sure justice. But he is ever with the pious and good, and he helped me find you and bring you to the righteous cleansing that has been ordained for you."

He grabbed a hank of red hair and hacked it with his blade. "No more can you tempt men with your sorcery, Witch," he said, shearing her close to the scalp. She whimpered, and I could see the blood and raw skin where he was careless. "Four husbands in the ground," he said. "Victims of your lust. Of your fire-kissed hair, your tender lips, your ample breasts." I could hear the longing in his voice. He desired her. He wanted to bury himself in that hair, those lips, those breast. He blamed her for his desire, his own lust. And because he couldn't have her, he would hack away all her beauty and tenderness and burn what remained.

I saw the long night of torture play in fast-forward in my head. The cutting, the branding, breaking, and ripping. I knew we couldn't stop it from happening. Her body was committed to this atrocity, and we were merely wraiths on the edge of the firelight. We weren't here to stop this. No, we were here to release her from her body.

The priest returned to the fire, placing his blade in the flame to render the metal red-hot. While he waited, he turned away from the naked woman and prayed, his rosary slipping through his fingers as he mumbled the words of his own incantation to the darkness.

I stepped into the firelight, Robin and Lilly at my side. I could feel the heat from the dancing flame. It seemed merry and cheerful, quite contrary to the dark purpose to which it was being set. I could feel the flame on my bare skin, smell the rot from the forest's fallen leaves and trees, see the pock marks on the priest's scarred and pitted face, hear the crickets and toads croaking their love songs into the damp night. I could perceive every sensory detail about this moment, and yet I was here without a body.

The priest couldn't see us. He believed so wholly that his God protected him from such astral specters that he blinded himself to our presence. The bound witch behind him, on the other hand, walked in both worlds, saw into both worlds. She looked at me with both fear and love.

"Rose?" she said, panic rising in her throat. "Robin?" She looked at Lilly, and some level of understanding settled on her face. "Petronilla, help me."

Ah. I suppose Lilly looked enough like her ancestor that Alice took her for the servant and coven-sister who had been executed just a few days earlier. I looked at Robin. "Does she think I'm her daughter?" He nodded, pain in his eyes. Okay. Well, I suppose it would do neither of us any good to convince her differently. Not right now, at least.

The priest sighed as he paused from his prayers. He hissed, "Silence, foul sorceress! Your coven will not save you from the fire, no matter how loud or long you plead. Your devils and daughters of Hell have no power here."

I held my finger to my lips in that familiar call for silence. In my other hand, I realized, was the flask of dwale. I held it aloft for her to see. "Dwale has found you," I said.

Tears welled in her eyes and rolled heavily over her cheeks.

"You are right to weep," sneered the priest. "But your penitence is too late. Only the fire can redeem you now."

We came in close to Alice, close enough to touch her flesh. Robin took the flask from me and held it to Alice's lips. She gulped it all down. With Alice, we didn't have to worry about dosage. The more the better. We were killing her mercifully compared to the so-called holy man with his fire.

Robin wrapped his arms around her and nuzzled her neck with his whole face while we waited for the potion to take hold. Lilly sang a lullaby as she stroked Alice's poorly shorn head. I knew the song, so I joined her, adding harmony to her melody.

Go to sleep, you little babe
Go to sleep, you little babe
Everybody's gone in the cotton and the corn
Didn't leave nobody but the baby

Don't weep, little babe
Don't weep, little babe
Honey in the rock and the sugar don't stop
Gonna bring a bottle to the baby

Go to sleep, pretty baby
Go to sleep, pretty baby
You and me and the Devil makes three

Don't need no other lovin' baby

Go to sleep, pretty baby
Go to sleep, pretty baby
Lay your bones and the alabaster stones
And be my ever-lovin' baby

Alice's eyes drooped, and she swooned where she sat. Her head rolled down to her chest and then snapped up and looked at us with such clarity that it startled me and Lilly out of our song.

"She's with us," Robin said.

"Do you mean she died?" Lilly asked.

"No," said Robin. "It will be a few hours before her body fails. But her spirit is free from that shell now. She won't feel what that monster does to her."

Alice looked at me and Lilly more closely. "You're not who I thought you were," she said. "Or you are, but you're different."

"Let us leave this awful place." Robin's voice was soft, apologetic.

Alice stood up, her spiritual body unfettered. She took a step forward. "I'll not look back at my breathing corpse for fear of being shackled in that unfortunate piece of crockery until it is finally shattered. Walk with me out of sight and sound of its breaking."

We walked with her back through the underbrush and along the trail into the enveloping darkness beyond the firelight. My eyes were struggling to adjust to the blackness of the forest, and I blinked hard several times. Blink, dark forest. Blink, dark temple room. Blink, moonlit meadow. Blink, temple room. Blink, dark seashore. My eyes focused on Robin's form which was silhouetted against the glowing sand. He was looking at the horizon. I looked at Lilly. But where was Alice?

"She is passing beyond the ninth wave," he said to my unasked question. Or maybe I had asked it after all. I couldn't recall.

"How did that happen already?" I asked, my throat dry and sticking with each word.

"It's been two hours," Robin said mildly.

I felt my eyes widen, betraying the disbelief I felt. Lilly's eyelids, on the other hand, were half shut. She was having an argument with someone I couldn't see.

"Our purpose being completed," Robin explained, "the effects of the belladonna are finding their way into your hallucination. The next several hours are going to be very strange."

Chapter 19

Strange was an understatement.

I lay that night and into the next day in the arms of Mistress Belladonna, the beautiful lady. Nausea hit me, but I never vomited. The nausea came in waves throughout the trip, each new iteration surprising me, having forgotten about the last.

I was thirstier than I'd ever been in my life. I felt like I had been dry roasting in the desert for three days. No matter how much water I drank, my thirst persisted. Robin took a bottle from me, warning me that I would make myself ill if I kept trying to drink away the dry-mouth.

I lost track of where I was. Sometimes I would know that we were in the temple room in my basement, but then I would drift into a confusion trying to remember when I brought trees or standing stones or a cave into the temple. Accepting it as the logic of a dream, I would think, "But this has always been here," and then I would sleep in that twilight slumber, open to whatever oddity was coming next.

When I woke astride Robin, his cock deep inside me, I was unsurprised. Of course, this was happening. This was always happening. There was never a time when he wasn't buried inside me, my hips grinding against his pelvis, his hand pleasuring Lilly's sacred cave, my mouth moaning into hers as we kissed. We were always this triangle of love and lust, longing and satisfaction. The moment was endless, eternal. I sank into it, letting the pleasure overtake me as the room filled with stars.

Without transition, we were in a meadow. The moon I had seen here earlier was gone, engulfed in brooding clouds. Flashes of lightening licked the sky and struck a willow tree fifty yards from us. I could smell the ozone. Lilly laughed and howled, spinning like a child with Robin, trying to see who would get dizzy and fall down first.

Except they'd already fallen. They fell eons ago, when the ziggurat temple in Babel was thought to touch the sky, and I was a priestess. The wife of the God. My flame colored hair curling around the cattle horns I wore with my crown. The flooding of my fertile river valley brought torrents to the Euphrates. My lusty banks over-flowed. The cup of my sex was over-filled by my mate, the river rushing to sweeten and ripen the earth.

The floods swamped the meadow. Lilly danced in the deluge, howling and screaming her wrath, her rage, her longing. Robin answered, his growl calming her, bringing her storm down low. Focused. She grabbed his hair and pulled him with her to the ground, rode him down. He howled and bucked his hips to plunge himself deeper.

The candles burned low in the temple. Robin and Lilly muttered in their half-sleep. I slipped into the dark, blank space between dreams, a storm finally dying outside our basement's half-buried concrete walls.

Chapter 20

A belladonna hangover is nothing to trifle with. *Hangover* can't even be the right word. It was recovery from poisoning. The dry-mouth lingered. My vision was blurry for a full twenty-four hours after I was finally able to peel myself off the floor of the temple room. I was sticky, though I assumed that had less to do with the dwale than it did our storm-inciting romp through Wonderland. And I had a fierce headache.

I tacked a heavy blanket up to the window of my bedroom to block the weak light that nevertheless battered my abused head, and Robin and I snuggled and snored our way through fifteen hours of recovery. A dreary rain splattered the world while we sheltered against the lingering effects of the hallucinogens.

Robin recovered faster than I did. He massaged my head with his strong fingers and sang me a quiet healing chant in a language I didn't quite recognize. It might have been Old English or Old German. He may have even been speaking in tongues, for all I knew. What I did know was that the meanings of the words were clear to me, even though the words themselves were foreign and strange. Robin called for the light within my body to shine and heal the darkness that lingered there. I saw a vision of a bird with the sun on its snowy wings, and when the bird flew into dark groves of trees, the light followed it.

When I woke up, morning was rousing herself into slow action. The world was blue outside the windows, and the day seemed in no rush to begin. I, on the other hand, couldn't stay in bed another minute. My body ached from lying down so long, and my mouth tasted like something had crawled into that little cave and died. Time for my most basic daily ritual of tinkling and toothpaste.

Robin wasn't in bed when I woke, so I wasn't surprised to find him in the kitchen. Nor was I particularly shocked to see Lilly. She had probably slept away yesterday, too. I was, however, surprised to see Grace awake before dawn. None of us were early risers, after all. She was bright-eyed and smiling, though, so I hoped that her wakefulness was just a peculiarity in schedule and not the byproduct of anxiety.

"Good morning, favorite people," I said to the room. "How did you all sleep?"

"Like I had been chased through the wilderness by dark faeries," Lilly said.

I chuckled. Yeah. That sounded about right.

"Peacefully and long," said Robin with a smile as he leaned down to kiss me hello. His steaming cup of coffee wafted its siren scent to my nose, and I moved to pour myself a cup.

"How about you, Gracie?" I asked. "We were all pretty out of it yesterday. Did you have a good day and night?"

She shrugged and said blandly, "I was lonely, but I figured you needed the sleep. You guys did quite a ritual the night before."

"Did we wake you with it?" I asked, concerned. "I have no idea how loud we may have been. I was hoping we didn't bother you."

She shook her head. "No, I didn't hear anything. I was woken up by that terrible storm, though."

Lilly gave a sheepish nod. "Yeah, I think that was me."

We all knew that Lilly's sorcerous specialty was weather magic, but she'd never produced any results quite that spectacular before. We looked at her, me with eyebrows arched, Grace with eyes wide, and Robin smiling.

"I didn't know you had that in you," I said. "That's impressive."

She shrugged and nodded, a shy but proud little grin curving her lips. "I haven't ever been the cause of a storm quite that big before," she said. "But when I was a teenager, I think I escalated a storm once when I was really pissed. It went from an average thunderstorm to being a tornado. Some people actually got hurt in it. An old woman died." The smile had completely vanished. Her brows were knitted together. "I kept a tight lid on myself after that, and I learned to focus my weather witching on decreasing violent storms and nudging them to areas where they would do the least damage."

We all nodded silently. I didn't know what to say. How do you comfort a friend who had inadvertently killed someone with her magic? You don't. Lilly had claimed accountability for her actions, and I could see that she had paid a price.

"I just hope nobody was hurt by this recent storm," she said.

Robin shook his head. "I don't believe they were."

Grace added, "No, I really don't think anyone was harmed, but you did create quite a stir. There was a minor storm system moving through this area before I even went to bed, but then this really fierce storm cell basically focused right here over our house. It extended maybe a mile in each direction around us. People have been talking about it online, and I guess there was a news report about it. It seems to defy all the meteorological rules. There were some downed trees, and a couple of power lines were taken out, but nobody was hurt that I've heard."

Lilly was visibly relieved. "Good. I didn't feel very much in control of myself."

"You were more in control than you think," Robin interjected. "You unleashed a mighty power, but it was concentrated and basically harmless. Well done, Lilly."

Lilly blushed and nodded, the room falling silent again.

"I've always liked how our covenmates have such a wide range of expertise," Grace said, enthusiastically. "Lilly is a potent weather witch. Evaline is a skilled shapeshifter. Pearl is such a talented healer."

"You are the best psychic I have ever known," I said to Grace.

She smiled and did her best to look humble, but her pride showed through the convention of humility. Grace knew she was good. She made a very tidy living from her skill as a psychic reader. She was one of the few psychics at her shop whose schedule was booked solid every day she worked. She had every right to be proud of herself.

"And you," Lilly said to me, finishing up the set, "are a gifted herbalist."

I nodded. Yes, I was definitely an herbalist, but I wondered if that was the special gift I brought to the coven.

"Rose in her garden," Robin said, looking at me with appraisal on his face, "is a benefit to all, but the herbalist's craft is a skill that all of the Wise may learn with relative ease. To bring forth healing from the soul, to call down the rains, to read the tapestry of a life's web, to change forms – these are all acts of sorcery, not just training."

Lilly and Grace nodded. I looked at the tablecloth, focusing on a yellow rose in the linen pattern. "Do I not have a sorcerous gift?"

Robin leaned across the table, taking my hand in his and looking me in the eyes. "Yes, my love," he said. "You are the Rose Beyond the Grave."

I blinked. "What does that mean?"

"Life in death" he said. "The light in the darkness, the rose beyond the grave." His eyes were unfocused now. He was looking at me and seeing the universe.

I still didn't understand what he was trying to convey, but a chill covered my scalp and shoulders. The hairs on my arms were standing on end.

His eyes snapped back into sharp focus, and he leaned back in his chair, releasing my hand. "What work have you done with the dead, Rose? What necromancies have you performed?"

I thought about his question for a moment. "Last night's ritual aside," I began, "I'm not sure. I mean, I like talking to spirits on the Ouija board, and I seem to have good success with it, especially when I work with Grace. I've always maintained an ancestor altar, and I have always loved graveyards. But that is about it."

"Hmmm," he said, looking at me through squinted eyes. "We may need to do some experimentation to prove or disprove my theory. Can you get out the board now?"

I looked at Grace. She and I always did this type of thing together. We were a very clear and frighteningly accurate channel when we worked together. Information came through more muddled when I worked alone or with a different partner.

The trouble was that Grace hadn't wanted to use the board with me much in recent months. She got tired and cranky every time we talked to spirits this way, and she had been refusing to engage at all lately. In fact, she wouldn't even do tarot readings for me or anyone else in the coven unless we pleaded.

So when I looked at her, the question was in my eyes. *Will you do this with me?* She shrugged one eyebrow and shoulder and gave a little nod. The gesture said, *I suppose*, with all the enthusiasm of agreeing to take out the trash.

I nodded to Robin with a "be right back." I went to my room to fetch one of my boards and planchettes. My little collection included six different types of talking boards and assorted pointers. I had the "William Fuld Talking Board Set" published by Parker Brothers that was iconic, but I also had a Cryptique board featuring a dark blue background and golden letters and two handmade boards. One was my own creation, and the other had been made for me by a friend several years ago. My fanciest board was a limited edition job made by a famous witchy artist. It came with its own velvet-lined wooden case. But my very favorite board, and the one I chose for this morning's session, was a 1940's Hasko board that had belonged to my step-grandfather. He was a Mason and a mystic, and I was proud to have his talking board as well as a crystal ball that had belonged to his mother.

I grabbed the board and the planchette that I had purchased online. The original pointer for this board had long since been separated from it. I took a steadying breath. *Grace may not be into this right now, but we'll still produce good results. And maybe I can talk with Robin about how to improve my skills in the future.*

When I returned to the dining room, the others had already cleared space at the table. I placed the board in the spot provided and set the planchette next to it. I had a rule about not touching the planchette to the board until we were ready to talk to a spirit. The friend who had introduced me to talking boards in college had once told me that the planchette was like an eye. When it was on the board, vision and voice went both ways between the spirit world and the physical one.

I reached for Lilly and Robin's hands, and they linked hands with Grace who sat opposite me. "We always start by calling our circles," I explained to Robin. "We usually just visualize them, but I'd like us to speak them this time."

He nodded, and we all closed our eyes.

"We call to the Circle of the Spheres – the realms above, below, and between," I began, my voice forceful with command and control. "Be here now!" I paused, feeling outside of myself with those innermost senses. I shivered when I felt the wall of energy. "The first circle is cast."

Lilly was the next to speak. "I call to the Circle of Gates – north and south, east and west. Throw open your doors and send forth your roads to meet in the middle of our compass. Be here now!" Another pause. Another shiver as the energy settled around us. "The second circle is cast."

Grace took a breath and spoke in a theatrical voice. "I call to the Circle of Watchtowers – castles of gold and silver, of stone and glass. Rise up and guard us from the cross-quarters. Be here now!" Pause. Shiver. "The final circle is cast."

I opened my eyes and was about to release hands when Robin spoke. "For we are the tree on the hill, the spiral castle that opens into every place. All the worlds are open to us. So mote it be."

"So mote it be," we said in unison.

The world continued to lighten outside our kitchen windows, and it wouldn't be long before the sun would rise somewhere behind the trees that surrounded our house. Inside the kitchen, the lights blazed, the scent of fresh coffee hung in the air, and the electricity of ritual zipped around the room.

I placed the planchette on the board which was oriented for me to read it easily. Grace rarely looked at the board when we worked. I asked the questions and read the answers. She seemed to know where to move the planchette to form those responses, although she wouldn't have known what was being said if I wasn't speaking the words aloud.

We'd each tried working with our coven sisters to see if we got similar results in other combinations. The short answer was no. We got some results, but nothing was as clear, efficient, or easy as when Grace and I worked the board together.

As we each laid the fingertips of our right hands on the planchette, I said, "We call into the spirit world, to that time out of time. We call to a spirit who wishes to speak with us, one who offers help and no harm to us and ours. We call to any positive spirit with information that will aid us in our current troubles."

We waited a moment. I could feel a force tugging at the planchette, not quite ready to move it. I looked at Rose who was looking down at the board, except that her eyes were shut.

The planchette moved. It went to the word *Hello* and then to the letter *S*.

"Is this the spirit we know as S?" I asked.

The planchette slid up to the *Yes* on the right-hand side of the board.

I looked at Robin. "We've talked with this spirit before," I explained. "She has only identified herself as S. Sometimes she answers in the affirmative with that letter, as well."

"She?" he asked, a twinkle in his eye.

"Oh." I realized I'd never asked the gender of the spirit before, and I'd never used a gender-specific pronoun in reference to S, either. "Are you a female spirit?" I asked the board.

There was a pause followed by a slow slide of the planchette to *Yes*.

"The answer I heard in my head was *Usually*," I said.

Grace nodded. "That's what I got, too."

"Were you a human person before you were a spirit?" I asked. I immediately felt foolish, given my own belief in the cycle of reincarnation.

Another pause. Then, *Yes*.

"What was your name?" I asked.

The planchette moved slowly, spelling out the words *I don't remember*. Another pause. *Too long*.

"It's been too long since you died?" I asked for clarity.

Yes.

I was asking the wrong questions, I realized. I could get this spirit's history some other time. We had asked for the help of a spirit who knew information that could help us with our current problems. Time to ask questions relevant to that thread of thought.

"Do you know something about Dr. Thomas Sewall or the people who are committing human sacrifice in Indianapolis?" I asked.

Pause.

I felt the pull in two different directions, and I realized I had asked two yes-or-no questions. "Sorry," I said. "Do you know something about Dr. Thomas Sewall?"

Yes. Guardians.

"That's right," I said. "He is the whacko preacher for the Guardians of Faith Ministries."

Bad man.

"You can say that I again," I said to the air.

Bad ...

"I was joking, S," I laughed. "You don't need to repeat it."

Stillness.

"So," I asked, "I think he's a bad man because he's starting a modern day witch hunt. But why do you think he's a bad man?"

A long pause. I could feel her gearing up for spelling out several words. When she started, they came faster than we were expecting. I struggled to keep up with translating the onslaught of letters into separate words.

Sewall is a dark power pretending to be light. He lies to the world. He has hurt children. One boy is dead.

Whoa.

"Did Sewall kill a boy?" I asked, hearing the stunning absurdity of the words.

No. Boy killed himself.

"Did Sewall do something to the boy that made him want to commit suicide?" I asked.

Yes. Rape.

I looked across the board at Grace. Her face was white with shock. Her hands were trembling.

"How old was the boy?" I really didn't want to know.

13.

I took a deep breath. I had suspected Sewall of being a dangerous monster, but I had certainly never expected anything of this nature.

"Is there any proof of this?" I asked. "Is there any way we can validate what you are saying or help the police catch him?"

More boys.

"He's done this to more boys?" I asked.

Yes. They will light the pyre to consume him.

I let that sit for a moment. I wasn't sure what else to ask.

Lilly asked, "Is there anything at all that we should do to speed this along?"

No. Justice coming soon.

Okay, then. I guess we would ride it out. I mean, we didn't have any actual evidence. I couldn't go to the police with accusations based on spirit communication with a talking board.

"Do you have any information about the person or persons responsible for the ritual murders in Indy recently?" I asked.

Hell's temple.

"Yeah," I agreed. "What they do is certainly hellish."
Bad witches.
"So they are witches, like us?" I asked.
Not like you. Evil. Mad with magic.
"Are they going to strike again?" I asked.
Even now.

A chill ran through me, and I saw everyone else shiver as well.

"What can we do?" I asked.
Robin and Lilly can find them.
Robin and Lilly sat at attention.
"How?" I asked.
Robin will search the witches' web for the hellish temple. They are snakes.

"And what will Lilly do?" I asked, still not sure that I understood what Robin was expected to do.
Lilly will search the other web.
"The internet?" I asked.
Yes.
"I feel pretty unclear about this, S," I said. "Is there anything else you can tell us?"
The demon they are calling. Scary. Must stop them.
"I agree," I said. "Am I right in thinking they are trying to manifest him the same way we manifested Robin?"
Yes. With death instead of life.
"But he will be here in physical form if they succeed?" I asked.
Don't let them succeed.
"We'll do our best," I said. "I hope we're able to figure this out."

The planchette moved painfully slow across the board.
Tired now.

Grace was sagging in her chair. Damn. I felt energized and ready to go. I could do this all day, but there was no point making life harder for everyone around me.

"Alright, S," I said. "Thank you for your help. We will do what we can with the information you gave us."

The planchette dragged heavily to *Goodbye*. I picked it up and sat it down next to the board.

Placing my hands on the board, I said, "This session is ended. The board is closed. The eye is shut."

Grace swayed in her chair. "I'm going to take a nap," she said. She stood without ceremony and walked out of the room.

"I'm going to start looking on the internet," said Lilly, and she bounded out of the room.

Robin and I looked at each other. "Do you have any idea how you're supposed to search the witches' web for these bad witches?" I asked.

"I have some thoughts," he said cryptically. "I'm almost at full strength in this form. I should be able to pin down this hellish temple of snakes within a day or two."

Oh, good. "What should we do in the meantime?" I asked.

He raised an eyebrow and grinned.

"More sexual healing?" I asked, feeling the giggle that fluttered unvoiced in my chest.

He nodded and stood, a distinct bulge evident in his pajama pants.

"I was hoping you'd say that," I giggled and ran toward my bedroom, enjoying the delicious panic of being chased.

Chapter 21

She cried without sound, the tears sliding up her face. She was suspended by her ankles from a metal structure that reminded her of the metal squat rack her husband kept unused in their garage.

She had been these people's captive for hours, but she had no memory of being taken. She had been eating concession stand nachos at her son's soccer game on the north side, and then she woke up here. She had no idea where *here* was. A garage or a storage building. It had one of those metal roll-up doors, and she had screamed in those first few hours, hoping they were close enough to neighbors or businesses that someone would hear her cries.

Her voice was hoarse now, and she had lost hope that she would be heard. These monsters had been abusing her for hours, unconcerned with any noise she tried to make. Her screams and cries delighted the woman, who laughed and derided her any time she showed a sign of pain, humiliation, or fear.

She hoped she would die soon. She knew it was coming. She had seen the news reports, and she rightly assumed that she was the third victim of this deranged cult. First the homeless man, then the hooker. She had felt sorry for them, but she never thought these killers would have come to her part of town and taken someone like her. They had chosen unconnected people before. People who were alone and desperate in the world.

She wasn't like the others. She had married her college sweetheart, an orthodontist named Tim. She lived in a nice house and good neighborhood. She had children.

Oh, God! The kids. Please, God, don't let them have my kids! She cried again, praying silently. She hadn't seen or heard the kids, nor had these monsters mentioned them. But she had been at her son's game with her daughter in tow. At the very least, the children would be frightened that their mother had disappeared.

One of the other soccer moms had to have noticed her departure. Someone would have called her husband, and maybe even the police, when she wasn't there to take the kids home. That would have been less than an hour after her abduction. Kids' soccer games just aren't that long.

It didn't matter. Nobody was going to find her before these robed bastards killed her. The things they had done to her, she wasn't sure her mind could survive even if her body was able to escape. Before they strung her up like a pig about to be butchered, they had broken her. She had been beaten, for sure. Probably raped, though she didn't have a clear memory of it. Still, she felt swollen and raw. She had a deep ache. She didn't need to remember the abuse to know that it had happened.

It was the woman's laughter that tormented her most. Laughter and humiliation. The last time she had screamed and struggled against her restraints, she was bound on the floor. The woman had acted like she was turned on by her struggle. She had hiked up her red robe and began masturbating, matching each scream and cry with her own aroused moan and grunt. The two men had followed suit, touching themselves. She stopped screaming but continued to sob as they had all stood over her and ejaculated on her body.

"We give this gift of primal lust and violence," the woman had crowed, "to that darkest king of the demons, whom we worship. Come closer, Lord, to the defilement of this innocent."

"*In nomine Satanas. Nema!*" the henchmen chanted.

"Draw strength from her weakness," the woman continued, "and glory from her humiliation."

"*Superbire et fortis.*"

155

"Come closer, Our King," she roared, "for you shall walk among us soon."

"*Sumite vires, Rex gehennam.*"

And now she hung, a symbol painted on the floor below her. She had seen that symbol on the news. She knew it was the signature of their demonic king. She knew that soon, her blood would flow from a slice or a puncture in her throat, roll down her face, and collect in a pool over that symbol. She knew, and she no longer cared.

Chapter 22

A police cruiser pulled into my driveway. I saw it from the living room window where I was sipping tea and working on my novel, Anyanka and Robin sprawled on the floor, daydreaming. I broke out in a cold sweat without fully understanding why my body thought I was guilty of something. My brain was waffling between internal screams of *"holy shit"* and *"I didn't do anything wrong."* It was the same reaction I have any time I see a cop at a speed trap. I rarely speed, so I have no real reason to feel like I'm about to get busted. I've never had a reason to fear the police, and yet I did. I really did.

Police officers on my lawn couldn't be here for anything good. Someone was hurt or in trouble. Whatever the police were here for couldn't be good.

I met them at the door. Outside the door, actually, with the door shut behind me. I may not have done anything wrong, but I wasn't inviting law enforcement personnel into my witchy abode without a warrant.

"Good afternoon, officers," I said to the two officers standing in the gravel driveway. My blood pressure was stabilizing, and I saw that the decals on the sides of the cruisers said Indy Metro. These weren't the local cops. Indy police couldn't arrest me in Monrovia, could they? Even with a warrant, wouldn't they need to be accompanied by local police? I had to be honest with myself. I had no freaking clue. All I could hope is that they didn't have a reason to arrest me. "How can I help you?" I asked.

One of the men stepped ahead of the other. They weren't wearing uniforms. I didn't know much more about the police than what I'd gleaned from *CSI* and *Dexter*, but I was thinking these were detectives. "Good afternoon, ma'am," he said. He flipped his badge out from under his jacket. "I'm Detective Jackson with the Indy Metro Police Department. That's Detective Schneider." He pointed at the younger man in the driveway. "Are you Rose Wheeler?" I nodded. "We have a couple of questions for you."

Gulp. "What about?"

He looked uneasy. "I'm assuming you're familiar with the ritualized murders that have been happening in Indianapolis."

I nodded. "I've been following them on the news, sure."

He held up a folder. "There was another incident last night."

Ice ran down my spine. "But why would that bring you here?"

He took a large photograph and a piece of paper from the folder and handed them to me. The color photo showed a woman hanging from her ankles, her throat slit, a pool of blood below her dangling corpse. Peeking out from the edge of the dark red blood were black markings that I knew were part of the demonic sigil.

I threw up. I'd never seen anything as horrific as this. I mean, yes, I'd seen horror movies that were actually much more graphic; but this was real. The woman wasn't an actor covered in fake blood. She had been a living person who had suffered through Gods-know-what and died like an animal in a slaughterhouse. And I was seeing it. On my porch.

So, yeah, I threw up over the railing into the shell garden.

Robin was at my side before I had a chance to regain any level of composure. "Rose, what happened?"

I could only shake my head. Tears stung my eyes. I was embarrassed and still queasy.

"I'll get you water and a cloth," he said, heading back into the house. I nodded and held onto the rail.

My mind was churning as much as my stomach. The picture was grotesque, but what was worse was the idea that this detective had brought it to my doorstep. I was sure I was about to learn why, and I was terrified that I was about to be another witch blamed for a crime I didn't commit. Me and Sondra Little.

Robin was back at my side with a glass of water and a small towel. I rinsed and wiped my mouth, as he helped me into a chair. The detective watched us, his face inscrutable.

When I was settled into my seat, he said, "This letter was found at the scene." He handed the piece of paper to me.

It took my eyes a moment to focus. I always found it hard to make sense of the written word when I was under pressure. I forced myself to breathe deeply and read slowly.

The letter was titled "Templum Chaldeos: Manifesto."

We are the witches of the Templum Chaldeos. We have worked in anonymity for years, living among the sheep of the Christ god, the false prophet of the Dead Age. You knew us not, nor did you dare to fear that we were among you.

We are as the witches of old, fornicating in your temples, consuming the flesh of your innocent children, tempting your daughters and sons into delicious defilements, ensnaring your wives and husbands in the perversions which you all publicly shun.

Indianapolis only knows us now because we have chosen to make it so. We have let you see a glimpse of the abominations we have perpetuated upon the trash of this city – the homeless, the hookers, the weak, pathetic, and ugly souls that you have thrown away. Now, we show you the desecration that has befallen so many of the innocents who have been victim of our Craft. Mothers and children have come into our loving embrace, even as this one did, their blood and pain and humiliation fueling our work.

We have sacrificed them in the name of our Dark King, who is rising even now from the depths of Hell to be with us, walking the world and spreading his wickedness. We are his whores, and there is no end to the lewd, licentious, and blood-thirsty acts we will perform with him at our sides.

Your fear is our fuel. You are fools, and we will be your masters.

To seal this work, we sacrifice three of our own to your mob. Work your good justice upon them, as we know you must. These three witches have been instrumental in the sacrifices you have already witnessed. They have laughed in your face on the courthouse lawn. They go now to the pyre that the city sets for them.

Before my eyes even reached the names, I knew my own was there. Why else would these detectives have come to my house?

Rose Wheeler

Grace McCutcheon

Evaline Morrow

"I'm not in any way affiliated with this hellish nonsense," I blurted before I could censor myself.

The detective pulled another picture from his folder. It was a black and white shot from the rally to save Sondra Little. I was standing at the center of the shot, my mouth open wide and my arms gesticulating. I believe it was the moment when I spoke to the assembled witches, just before we raised energy. Evaline and Robin were flanking me.

"This is Evaline Morrow, isn't it?" he asked, pointing at Evie. "And Grace McCutcheon is your roommate."

"I think I need a lawyer," I said.

He shifted his weight. "You have that right, of course; but you are not being charged. At this time, we don't have any solid reason to suspect that the letter is anything more than an attempt to shift attention onto a set of known witches."

I nodded. "Yeah," I said. "I think the other women you have in custody are victims of that same scapegoating."

He looked up at the cobwebs hanging from my front porch light. "We're hoping you might have some information that can lead us to the actual culprits."

My eyes narrowed as I tried to make sense of what was happening. "Are you asking me for a consult?" I asked. "Like the psychics who help with murder investigations on television?"

He shifted his weight and looked at the deck boards under his feet before meeting my eyes again. "Look, Ms. Wheeler," he shrugged, "this is all very unorthodox. All of it. Most of us only found out about witches and magic within the last few years, and most people still aren't sure if it's even real. We've got bodies in coolers and the threat of some big bad bogeyman coming our way, and Indy Metro PD doesn't have a protocol for handling that."

Yeah. Me, neither.

"My sergeant wants this handled like any other murder investigation," he continued, "but the chief wants us to get on top of this whole magic thing as soon as possible. Chief wins."

This was more information than I would have thought a detective would give to the likes of me, but okay. I decided to just go with it. I made the snap decision to take him at his word and pray that I didn't end up in jail because of it. My naïveté had gotten me in trouble in the past, but I had the sense that this guy was being straightforward with me. It was a risk, but I figured I should go ahead and take it. Maybe having the ear of the police department was exactly what my coven needed.

"How can I help?" I asked.

He broke into a wide smile and then opened his folder.

I interrupted before he had a chance to start speaking again. "This will probably be easier inside," I said, opening the door. Robin shot me a questioning look. I shrugged. "We might as well sit in a warm room with a table and tea," I said.

I led the way to kitchen and offered them a cup of tea. They declined, which really didn't surprise me. I'm a known witch, after all. One of the Greek words for "poisoner" had gotten translated as "witch" in the King James Version of the Bible. No doubt, these men weren't entirely sure that I wouldn't slip a little something into their peppermint cuppa.

I put the kettle on anyway.

Jackson sat at the table with his notepad and pen poised for action. "Sir," he said to Robin, "may I ask what your relation is to Ms. Wheeler and her coven?"

Oh, please don't ask too many questions about Robin, I thought. *I don't even know if that man has proper DNA. I sure as shit can't explain about him.*

Robin answered, in his deliciously accented and easy manner, "I'm Rose's guest and friend, and I'm a friend to her coven."

Jackson jotted notes. "And your name?"

"Robin Artisson," he said. Jackson jotted that down, too.

"This is uncharted territory for me, Ms. Wheeler," he said. "In some ways, I'm not sure where to begin. There is so much that law enforcement doesn't know about the occult. We don't know what to expect, for instance, in terms of the magic itself. What is possible? What isn't? For instance, is it really even a possibility that the coven responsible for these murders can actually raise a demon to walk the streets of Indianapolis?"

I took a deep breath. "Under normal circumstances," I began, "I would say that it wasn't likely. Physical manifestation of a spiritual being is extraordinarily difficult to accomplish. It takes a great deal of skill and energy."

He scribbled and waited for me to continue. He could hear the "but" in my voice.

"I don't know about the skill of the coven in question," I said, "but I know they have gathered a great deal of energy. Enough that my own coven is worried."

"How do you know they have generated this energy?" he asked.

I twisted my lips as I tried to decide how to explain. The teapot whistled, and I busied my hands with making two cups of peppermint and lavender tea while my mouth found the words. "This whole city," I began, "the whole state, in fact, is obsessed with these murders. We're getting national attention, even. Every time a reporter shows the demon's symbol, says his name, and generally stirs up fear in their audience, that fear is getting fed into the magical working to bring him up. And not just the fear, but the revulsion and the hatred that is being generated, too."

Robin added, "And that is to say nothing of the dark hearts throughout the land who are hoping these witches are successful in their operation. No doubt there are some sympathizers in the audience who are lending their sick hope to this being's conjuration."

I brought Robin his tea and took my own seat at the table. The fragrance of the lavender and mint steamed up to my nose. I took a deep breath and felt at least one of my forehead creases relax.

"Do you have any idea who is behind these murders?" Jackson asked.

I shook my head. "No, not yet."

"Not yet?" he asked. "Is this something you are actively looking into?"

"In our own way," I answered. "Yes, we are trying to figure this out, too. It's in our best interests to stop this from happening. The murders are garnering nothing but fear and hatred for witches everywhere, and this demon rising would be bad news for us, as much as for you."

"I need to warn you that you could get in a lot of trouble if you are interfering with a police investigation," he said sternly.

I nodded. "We are aware of that, detective. Our methods are strictly spiritual, though, and I don't believe they could be seen as interference."

He looked dubious. "Like I said, this is all new territory for us. Who knows what will be considered interfering and what won't?"

I nodded. "Understood."

Jackson gathered his papers. Schneider, who had been conspicuously silent, stood and said, "We also ought to warn you that the manifesto you read outside was leaked to the press. There could be ramifications for you. Be careful and keep an eye out for trouble."

Jackson had the look of apology about him. "May I ask a favor of you and your coven, Ms. Wheeler?" he asked.

"Ask away," I said.

"If you do get wind of anything related to the perpetrators of these murders," he began while handing me a business card, "can you please contact me immediately?"

"I doubt anything we get will be admissible in court," I said.

"Let me worry about that," he grinned. "Right now, I'm more concerned with stopping these monsters." He paused for a moment and looked at me as if he was deciding how much to say. "There are some details about this last murder that we haven't given to the press. The woman who was murdered last night," he paused, "her two children are missing, as well."

"Holy shit," I muttered. "*Mothers and children*, they said. Fuck!"

He nodded. "Our top priority is to get those kids back alive, if we can. As for the courts, this case could change the nature of what is and isn't admissible."

"Uncharted territory," I echoed.

Chapter 23

"Rose?" I recognized Jason's strong Kentucky accent on the phone even without the help of his picture staring happily from my phone screen.

"Hi, Jason," I said. "What's up?"

"I'm so sorry, Rose, but I'm calling to let you know that we've had an emergency here at the store." Jason was the manager of the New Age store where Grace works. I could hear the strain in his voice, and I felt that icy chill pour down my spine again. Before I could ask what happened, he said, "Grace was shot a few minutes ago by a crazy woman who came in yelling about witches."

"What the fuck?" I said. "Oh my God. Ohmygod, ohmygod. Is she okay? I mean ...." I couldn't bring myself to ask if she was alive.

Robin was already at my side, and I could hear Lilly running up the stairs. I guess my panic was loud enough to get everyone's attention.

"I'm no doctor, but it looked like an in and out shot through her arm," Jason said. "She's not in mortal danger, I don't think. She was taken to Community South Hospital, just down the road."

"Okay, I'm on my way now," I said. "Is everyone else okay?"

He paused, and I could feel the fear releasing from his body, sending him into shivers. "Yeah, more or less," he said. "Nobody else was injured, and John tackled her before she shot a second time." John was one of the other psychics. "Rose, she was definitely targeting Grace. She had a print-out from some site online that has this crazy letter with both of your names and pictures."

165

A wave of dizziness washed over me. Robin caught my shoulders and helped me sit down.

"I just saw a copy of that letter, myself," I said. "A cop came by with it. Just left in fact."

"I'm so sorry this is happening to you," he said. "We know you didn't do this."

"Thanks," I said, blankly. "I'm going to get out the door now. I gotta get to Grace."

I gave Robin and Lilly the crib notes version as we gathered shoes, purses, and phones and left the house. Lilly offered to drive, but I needed my hands on the wheel, my mind focused on something other than Grace terrified and covered in her own blood.

The drive from my house to the hospital in Greenwood would normally have taken about forty minutes. I don't remember speeding beyond reason, so I think we must have bent the space-time continuum. We arrived at the ER in twenty-five minutes.

And then we waited. The doctor was finishing up with her. It may have been a relatively clean shot, but no gunshot wound is without risk of infection and a need for stitches.

Two hours slid by on the uncomfortable waiting room chairs, and we still hadn't heard anything.

"I'm sure she's going to be okay," Lilly said, holding my hand. "Jason said it wasn't that bad, for a gunshot wound."

"Jason is a retail manager and a psychic," I retorted. "I'm not sure how much experience he has with this type of thing."

Robin rubbed his hand across my shoulder, sweeping my hair to the side. "Don't borrow trouble, Rose," he said. "We'll know something soon, and I am certain that she is not in mortal peril."

I shook my head, the tears streaming down my face. My anxiety was ratcheted up so high I couldn't calm myself down again. Not easily. "This is our fault," I said. "Grace was shot because her name was on that fucking letter. Her name was on that letter because we got involved. We went to that rally. We stuck our big noses right into the middle of the mess."

Lilly and Robin stared at me while I railed.

"Don't you remember, Robin?" I asked. "She refused to go with us because she was worried about the repercussions. She tried to keep out of this, and now she has been shot because I wouldn't listen to her."

I could see a conflict forming on Robin's face. "Yes, we have chosen to get involved," he said. "But Grace was part of the ritual to bring me forward. She knew that I would be a champion for your protection. That was the point of my being manifest."

"Yeah," I said, "but that was against Sewall. Not this crazy coven, Templum Chaldeos, or whoever they are."

"Yes," he said, an edge of harshness glinting from the patience he was trying to offer me. "But I told you then that the attack would come on two fronts, and she was part of asking for my help. When this coven called me, I have to assume you knew there would be risks. You can't stand against bullies and oppressors and think no blows will fall upon your own heads."

I was fighting hyperventilation, which I knew was more likely to cause a breathing fit. I laid on the floor, my hands sprawled above my head, and forced myself to take deep, slow breaths.

"Robin is right," Lilly said gently. "Grace got cold feet, but we had already stepped in as a group to protect the witches of this city and do the right thing. Robin has given us some shelter – more than we would have had on our own. But we all knew we might get our hands dirty."

I nodded, tears sliding down the side of my face and into my hairline.

"We're here for Grace McCutcheon," I heard a woman's voice say at the check-in counter.

I vaulted off the floor, wiping the tears away and trying to regain the illusion of composure as I walked over to the woman and her husband. I recognized them as Grace's parents. We had only met a couple of times, but I was sure they would remember me.

"Mel. Dan," I said. "We haven't heard anything yet, but you're welcome to wait with us."

They stared at me, expressionless.

"I'm so sorry this is happening," I said. "I'm so worried about Grace."

Still no expression from either of them. They looked back at the receptionist who was sliding their ID's across the counter. "You can follow me," the woman said. "She's ready to be discharged."

"Wait," I muttered. "I don't understand. I've been sitting here for two hours with no word, and she's ready to go home? I could have ..."

Mel cut me off, her words squeezing between tight lips. "You are not her family, young lady," she said. "I don't care how close you think you are, you will never be her family. Grace is coming home with us."

Her dad, who was almost always silent, added, "I think you'd best go on home yourself, Rose. Grace doesn't want to see you."

I stood there, struck dumb, as the nurse escorted them beyond the security doors to where Grace waited for her parents.

Chapter 24

Lilly and Pearl are probably the best friends I've ever had. I knew that was true now more than ever. Yes, of course, we had shared deep belly laughs, irritations against minor foes, and even the occasional peevishness with each other, and still come out the other side as friends. Pearl and I had even known each other long enough to have disagreements that resulted in months of not speaking to each other. But returning home from the hospital without Grace, and being comforted by these two women let me know that they would always be by my side.

Pearl took the role of bad cop in today's game. "Fuck that," she blurted. "I mean it. I love Grace, and all, and she will always be family, but there is only so much of this that she can blame on us. Not much at all, in my opinion." She took a breath. "Am I sad for her that she got hurt? Yes. I'm I worried for her? Hell yes. But did you or I or Robin throw her in front of a lunatic with a gun? Hell no. I hope a few weeks at her parents will help her recover, more than just in her body." She added, with a cheekier-than-usual heart salutation, "Namaste."

I wanted to smile, but I was just so numb. I didn't feel the smile past the place in my brain that was immediately tickled by Pearl's bluntness. I wasn't actively crying, but my face felt swollen and tear-streaked from the hours I'd spent sulking during the day since I had come back to the house that Grace and I probably no longer shared.

That was actually a point of confusion and frustration. Grace wasn't really talking to me, but that meant that I didn't really know what was going on. Was she coming back after she recovered? Was she going to send her parents to collect her things, or did she intend to return after her mind and body recuperated from the trauma of her attack?

Rue, her slinky black cat, leapt into my lap. I petted her shiny fur, telegraphing the message, *I don't know if she's coming for you or not. Maybe you're my kitty now.*

"I know it's not the same," Lilly said, "but she left us, too, Rose. We're all in this together. We all made the decision to call Robin, to get involved. All of us. Even Grace. And her being hurt, in body and spirit, is hitting all of us hard."

I nodded, Rue purring in my lap. "I know. I'm just worried," I said. "I don't want her to be hurt, and I can't change that she is. I don't want her to be shutting us all out, and I can't fix that, either. I don't know what's going to happen with her or the coven or my relationship with her." I shrugged lamely again. "Things haven't been great lately, and now they may never be. I don't feel ready to be done trying with her, but that decision isn't just mine to make."

We all sat in silence for a moment. Each of us was staring at a different focal point.

The front door banged open, and in blew Evaline. Rue leapt from my lap, digging her back claws into my leg to better launch herself toward safety.

"You aren't going to believe this," Evie said breathlessly. "I've been trying to call you all, but nobody answered."

We reflexively checked our phones. "I don't have any signal," I said. "Me, either," echoed Lilly and Pearl.

"Fucking boonies," sighed Evaline. "I hope I can pull up one of the articles on my phone." She started fussing with the touch screen of her smartphone.

"Articles about what?" I asked. My curiosity was more than a little piqued.

No answer. She just kept tapping and scrolling on the screen.

"You're killing us, here," Lilly said. "What's going on?"

Evaline sighed and shoved her phone onto an end table in disgust. Her eyes were wide and twinkling when she spoke. "The *Right Honorable Reverend Doctor* Thomas Sewall has been arrested," she announced to gasps of glee.

"Wow, really?" Pearl said. "Hot damn!"

"For what?" I asked at the same time.

"For kiddie porn," Evaline said.

We all responded with grimaces and groans of disgust.

"Yep," Evaline explained. "Some grown nephew of his came forward with allegations of pedophilia and molestation, and he said there were pictures and videos on the minister's computer. Evidently, he was telling the truth because the bastard was hauled off in handcuffs from his church this morning."

"Whoa," I said. "I'm sorry for his nephew and the kids involved, but I am so glad that nut-job is out of our hair." And then I flashed on his congregation. "He is out of our hair, don't you think? Him and his zealous followers?"

Evaline shrugged. "Can't say for sure, just yet. But yeah, they seem to have taken a step back from him and his pet causes. They released a statement a few hours ago that basically said they were shocked to discover his perversions and abuse and they would be reevaluating the direction of the Ministry's missions."

"Well, thank-fucking-goodness," Pearl said. "We needed some good news today."

Chapter 25

"I'm ready for the final battle of this war," Robin announced, a little dramatically by my calculations. Maybe the proclamation just seemed out of place in my bright kitchen while Lilly and I cleared dinner dishes. "What skill and power I have are fully available to the coven in the cause of freedom."

We both stopped what we were doing to focus on Robin. Remnants of roasted squash and Brussels sprouts slid down the plate I was now holding limply over the scrap bowl.

"That's awesome, Robin," Pearl said, coming in from the living room. She and Evaline had been with us all day, talking about the new developments and sharing a little dinner and wine. "What does that mean? What can you do?"

Pearl and Evie took seats at the table, and Robin joined them. Lilly and I moved the dishes from the table to the counter so we didn't have to hold our witchy war council over the remains of fish and veggies. I refilled the wine glasses before sitting down across from Robin.

"I can locate the perpetrators of the sacrificial slaughter, for one thing," he said. "I already have a vague sense of where they are and when they intend to perform their final rite. With a little focus, I can pinpoint the needed details."

We all nodded our impressed approval.

"And then what do we do?" Lilly asked. "I mean, do we call the police immediately, or go check it out, or what?"

"Yeah," I said. "I don't know that the police are going to jump on a witch tip that comes from the ether. Plus, this is untested for us, too. Maybe we should go check things out to make sure we have the right place before we get law enforcement involved."

The other women shrugged and were silent. This was all new ground for us. We really didn't know what would be believable, appropriate, or even safe.

"In the old days," Robin said, "witches governed themselves. Most individuals and covens answered only to themselves, and it was rare for one to intervene in the affairs of another. There were times, though, when a witch or coven drunk with power or mad from despair would raise the ire of the others. Before too much damage was done, the offending witches would be silenced and stilled within the strictures of the Craft."

A mute chill ran through the room. "Is that what we are doing?" asked Pearl. "Are we going to kill these other witches?"

Robin offered a gentle smile. "These times are different," he said. "I believe that your police will be willing to investigate a tip that helps them catch the people responsible. They seem ready to accept help from wherever it comes."

I nodded. I certainly had that impression from the detective who questioned me. If we could bring him something solid, I think he would move fast to bring the killers into custody. We might be able to do this with minimal risk to ourselves.

"So, the plan is to discover their location, do a little reconnaissance to make sure we have the right place, and tip off the Indy police without getting caught up in the middle of things?" Lilly recapped.

"When you say it like that, it sounds really cloak-and-dagger," I said. "And also unlikely that we will get out of it unscathed."

"Well," said Pearl, "I think we've already been scathed." She raised an eyebrow at her own word choice. "I mean, we've already been hurt, as a group. Grace was shot and is possibly gone from us. That's a loss. But we shouldn't stop now. We have the chance to actually do some good. We can help. We have to try."

We all nodded.

"Let's not forget, either," Evaline added, "that at least one person at Indy Metro is open to getting a tip from us. As soon as we have any info, Rose should call that cop."

I nodded. I had already put Det. Jackson's number in my speed dial.

"Robin," I said, "what can we do if we find ourselves in a dangerous scenario with these other witches? This isn't the movies or a role-playing game. We aren't going into a wizard's duel with telekinetic defenses and magic missiles. None of us have any real-world fighting skills, and our opponents have proven themselves killers."

"Three times," Lilly added.

Robin looked at his hands and said, "Yes, they are killers, but I do not believe they are warriors. They are hunters, stalking and snaring their prey. The have chosen weak and unsuspecting victims. You are neither of those things."

Pearl made a fierce face and held her hands up in a "karate chop" gesture. "Yeah, they shouldn't mess with us."

Robin smiled indulgently and then said, "Even so, you are not without magical defenses and weapons. For one thing, your magic has increased by my weakened presence. It will increase even more now that I am strong. There are things we can do to make your magic more palpable."

"For tonight?" I asked.

He nodded. "Yes, for tonight."

"Like what?" I asked. "Let's get started."

Robin sat for moment before standing abruptly. He gathered all our wine glasses into the middle of the table. "When you take your vows of initiation, you share your blood with each other, yes?"

We nodded. I said, "It isn't direct sharing, but we all cut or prick our fingers and hold them to the oathstone, the anvil."

"A witch's power is connected through blood to other witches," he explained. "You are all connected to the Father and Mother of the Craft. Their power is in your blood. So far, though," he paused, looking pointedly at each of us, "that connection has only been called upon in the most metaphorical sense. Tonight, I will connect you to the source more directly."

He took a small, red pocket knife from his jeans' pocket and flicked the bright blade open. When he poked the tip of his finger, a little well of blood sprange almost instantly to the surface. *Sharp blade,* I thought. We generally used diabetic lancets to prick our fingers for oaths, but if I was going to use a blade, I wanted a scalpel-sharp one.

Robin tipped his finger over each glass, letting a drop or two mix with the sweet, local red wine we all favored. Then he handed the knife to Lilly.

I could see her pause. I felt the tension ripple around the circle of the kitchen table. I imagined that I could hear us each having the same internal debate. *But it's unsanitary! Cutting ourselves with the same knife. Drinking each others' blood. And it's a little weird. But ... well, I guess we are already intimate with each others' bodily fluids. We have sex with each other, and we've all had sex with Robin. We have all been tested in all the ways that matter. Okay. I can do this.* And Lilly cut her finger and squeezed her blood into each cup. Evaline and Pearl followed suit, as did I, without further hesitation.

Robin held his hands over the glasses and chanted something in a language I didn't recognize. When he finished, he picked up his own glass in salute.

"The line of Cain," he said, each of us now holding our glasses aloft, "is the red thread that encircles your waist in the symbol of your cords and encircles your hearts in your living blood. Red is the wine, and red is the blood that we share with the God of the Craft."

With that, we clinked glasses and drank to the bottom of our cups.

As the glasses clinked, I flashed on the image of a blue and white star surrounded by a red circle, and I was immediately aware that the five of us at the table made a lovely pentagram bound, now and always, in blood.

I didn't taste the blood in the wine, but I felt it. Every molecule of my being seemed to shine with its own interior light. I felt a thrum, a pulse of energy from deep within myself, and I felt the echo of that power from each person at the table. Robin seemed haloed in a red-gold glow.

I had no words to describe or even acknowledge this moment. I possessed a profound knowledge of the strength and ability within myself and my sisters. We could do this. I felt certain of it. We could find and stop the evil that threatened to arise bodily in our city.

"Where do we find them?" I asked Robin. "Where are they now?"

"I need a map," he said. "I know where they are, but I don't know how to tell you. I can only show you."

I found an old Indianapolis street-finder map in my parents' junk drawer. It had been there since they switched to GPS. Robin flipped the map to the page he needed and pointed. It was on the south side of town. I didn't know much more than that. We would just have to show up and see what there was to see.

Chapter 26

He and his sister had been kept in a wire cage for the two days since they had been snagged at the soccer game.

The lady in the red coat had told the coach that she was a friend of their mom's. Most of the other kids and parents were already gone. The coach had asked a few questions and seemed satisfied with the answers. Their mom had left the game to run a quick errand, she had said, but got sick while she was out. She called her friend to come pick up the kids and bring them home. She even knew their address.

They hadn't gone home, though. The lady's friend had given him and his sister a shot when they pulled out of the parking lot, and he had woken up in the cage. His sister had been slumped on his lap, her pants wet from where she'd peed in her sleep.

In the two days since they'd woken up, they hadn't left the cage. His nose crinkled at the stink, and he cast a sidelong glance at the corner of the cage they had been using as a toilet.

His little sister looked up at him, her eyes swollen from crying. He could feel that his own face was puffy and tender, too. He'd tried not to cry, but it was impossible. Every time the lady in red came to the cage, she said something horrible as she shoved a piece of bread or a bottle of water through the slot. And he cried.

"Good news, little lambs," she said, her voice not half as gentle as her words. "Tonight is the night you join your mom. Are you ready to leave this cage?"

His sister nodded vigorously. "I wanna go home. I want Mommy and Daddy."

The lady grinned, and he was afraid of her teeth. She didn't look like she was really smiling, more like she was about to take a bite. "Well, come on out and get ready," she said. "We need to get you out of these filthy clothes, first. Would you like a bath?"

"We just want to go home," he said. "We'd rather have our bath there."

The lady's smile vanished in an instant. "Well, you're taking it here."

She snatched them by their arms and pulled them out of the cage, trotting them to a small pantry or closet with a bare bulb in the overhead socket and a large tin basin on the floor. "Now, strip off those rags and wash yourselves," she barked.

They didn't move. He had never been naked in front of anyone except his parents before. That was bath time, too, but nobody had given him a bath for a year or two. He was big enough to do it by himself now.

"Now!" she shrieked. "Don't you dare make me do it for you. I promise you won't like it if I have to help."

His sister started crying and whimpering again. He looked at his own clothes and at hers. They were stiff in places. Soiled and smelly.

"It's okay, Sissy," he whispered gently. "I'll help you. It's okay."

She continued to cry, but she complied. In a moment, they were both naked. He covered his privates with his hands, but his sister's arms hung limply at her sides as she wept.

"Now wash," the lady demanded.

The water was cold. There wasn't enough room for them both to get into the metal tub. He took the single washcloth and bar of soap and tried to show his sister what to do. She wouldn't do it for herself, though. She just stood there crying and looking at the dirty concrete floor. Snot ran freely from her nose.

"Sissy, please," he begged, but before he could try to wash her himself, the lady marched up to them and pulled the little girl off her feet and dunked her in the tub. She choked and spluttered as the water splashed into her nose and mouth. "Hold your breath," the lady snipped before shoving his sister's head under the water.

"No!" he screamed, lunging at the woman. "Let go of her!"

Footsteps ran from the other room, and someone soft and bulky grabbed him from behind, pinning his arms to his sides. "No!" he yelled again and again.

The woman swiped roughly at his sister's face and body with the washcloth he had dropped. The little girl wailed and thrashed in the water, and the lady in red slapped her hard across the face. The shock silenced the girl, and the boy stood dumbstruck for a moment in his captor's arms.

"You brats need to learn the value of silence," she hissed. "No more screaming and flailing about! I can't stand it. Shut up, or I will truly give you a reason to cry and scream."

She yanked the girl out of the tub and led her by the arm out of the room. She muttered to herself, "Of course, I'm going to give you plenty of reasons to scream before this night is over."

Chapter 27

"Have you noticed that the rituals have happened in all four quarters of the city?" Lilly asked in the van as we pulled into an alley around the block from where Robin said we would find the coven. The buildings in this area were mostly industrial, and several had signs announcing their availability for lease. "First the east side, then the west. The mother of the kids was on the north side, and here we are on the south side for the children."

"Yeah," I said. "I'd noticed."

"If the demon is given the chance to rise," Robin said, "he will come from the middle of the crossroads."

I pictured the Soldiers and Sailors Monument downtown. It was a gleaming white obelisk of Indiana limestone that stood about fifteen feet shorter than the Statue of Liberty. It was at the literal and figurative heart of the city. Meridian and Market Streets crossed where it stood, and a circular drive surrounded it. That was the crossroads of the Circle City, and the monument was the stang.

I shuddered. "We have to stop this thing from happening. We just have to."

None of us had even discussed what might happen if the Templum Chaldeos, or whatever they were called, were successful. We didn't give voice to the horrors that we each imagined. Speaking our fears aloud would only strengthen their power and feed energy toward the goal that we were trying to thwart.

We got out of the van and walked silently behind Robin. I noticed for the first time that we were all dressed in black. Even through the anxiety that roiled in my belly, I snickered. Lilly shot me a questioning look. I shrugged and whispered, "We look like a newbie crew of cat burglars or something. We look really sketchy."

She laughed and nodded. "Yeah. We look more like a Goth band than a coven right now."

We both snickered, and the others all gave us the stink eye. Sometimes Lilly and I fell into fits of laughter together, and nerves only made it worse. We looked away from each other and stifled the giggles that always came when we tried to be serious.

Robin stopped short and put his hand up. He motioned for silence and pointed to a plywood covered window on the dingy concrete block building in front of us. The window was behind a large, leafless bush. He gestured for us to scoot deeply into the shadows and wait while he checked out the window.

All my nervous giggles had vanished, and I sunk as deeply into the shadows as I could. I could feel my sisters, but even I could barely see them, tucked as they were into the deep pools of shade afforded by awnings and doorframes. No moonlight gave them away, and the streetlights' weak glow didn't reach this far down the alley.

Robin came back and nodded, his handsome face grim in the eerie light. I took out my phone and texted Det. Jackson, as we had planned. I typed the address and added, *It's happening now. Please hurry.*

Robin leaned in close to my ear and whispered, "I don't think we can wait for the police to arrive. They've already started their ritual, and I don't know how long we have before those children are slain."

My phone was still in my hands, and the screen flashed to notify me of a new message. I jumped, startled by the sudden brightness but grateful I had remembered to turn the ringer completely off. *Stay put. On my way.*

I gulped. *Can't wait,* I replied. This could get us into so much trouble. Obstruction of justice was the least of the charges I saw in my future. If we failed, we might even get charged as accomplices.

There was no help for it. I couldn't stand outside these walls twiddling my thumbs while two kids were gutted inside. I beckoned everyone close enough to hear me whisper. "I think we have to go in. I won't blame anyone for choosing to stay out here, but I feel like I have to do what I can. The police will be here soon, so we're really only trying to disrupt the ritual and keep those kids alive until the cavalry arrives."

"I'm going in with you," Lilly whispered.

"Me, too," Pearl said.

Evaline nodded, a dark light burning in her soft brown eyes.

I looked at the door and back at my coven. "So, I've never thought to ask if any of you can pick a lock."

Evaline pulled a small pouch out of her back pocket. "I thought we might need this." She winked at me, and I could see her smirk despite the gloom. I made a mental note to ask Evie why she had a lock picking kit after this was all over. "I haven't always been a good girl," she said by way of explanation.

Good enough for now.

We followed her to the door and watched intently as she performed this strange new magic. The door clicked open, and I said a silent prayer that it wouldn't squeak while we eased it wide enough to slip past. In my mind, I saw the energy shield surrounding the ghoulish witches inside. I saw it crackle and spark, and in that moment I knew how to use it against them. I focused my will on adding a cushion of silence around the circle, like insulation. Little noises made out here wouldn't be audible to the people inside the circle.

The door didn't squeak, either.

Evaline led the way through the labyrinthine building. It looked like an old machine shop of some sort, but the machines were all gone. False walls, empty shelves, and metal structures that seemed entirely random to me formed obstacles to our goal. The door we entered was only about forty feet from the window through which Robin had heard the ritual begin. We were led back toward the front of the building and then diverted toward the far wall before Evaline discerned a path toward the children and their captors. How she was finding the path, I wasn't sure. She stopped once or twice to sniff the air, and she halted the whole group once when a rat scuttled across the hall some distance ahead.

As we rounded what I hoped was our last corner, I saw the flickering glow of candles casting strange shadows on the walls and floor. I heard a woman's voice, exultant and sensual. She was speaking a string of Latin that was muffled to my ears by the boxes and shelves and odd hunks of metal that still stood between us and them. Two or three deeper voices chanted in hushed and sonorous tones.

My pulse was racing. *Fuck! What am I doing? What were we thinking? We must be all insane.*

A child screamed, and we all pushed forward until we could see into the room. We were shielded from sight by the same shelves and abandoned equipment that had twisted and turned us in a serpentine dance all around the building. Their candlelight illuminated them and blinded them the same way stage lights illuminated actors on a stage. I knew from experience that they couldn't see anything beyond the reach of their little lights.

I wanted so badly to leap into the room, but my caution and terror told me to look before I jumped into this fight. I could feel the same tension in the women at my sides. I reached my energy out to touch Robin's, to check in with him. Unlike the rest of us, he felt clear, strong, and ready. He felt huge. I turned to look at him, half expecting him to be ten feet tall. Nope. Still a little over six feet, but I could see a darker outline that was monstrously large with horns like a ram curling around its head. *Hi there, Robin,* I thought. The shadow nodded.

I looked back toward the horror show in front of us. Two naked children were tied to metal frames facing each other. They trembled with cold and fear, dirty rags crammed into their mouths to stifle their cries. The boy had black wax hardening on his belly. In the poor light, I could see a red welt peeking out from below the wax. The woman who was crooning her Latin incantation held a black pillar candle in her red-gloved hands. She turned away from the boy and continued chanting as she poured black wax onto the sigil that filled the ritual circle. Her gaze shifted to the girl who shrieked like a caught rabbit.

"Stop!" Robin's voice boomed.

Evaline lunged forward, a snarl transforming her pretty face into something untamed and angry. Lilly and I flanked her, Pearl to my right, shaking with rage and fear. "Get away from them you crazy bitch," she screamed.

The woman was stunned for a moment, but only for a moment. She laughed, and the sound was throaty. "I'm so glad you could make it," she said. "And here I thought you had a previous engagement with the police."

"Yeah, not so much," I sneered.

The woman's eyes widened as I felt Robin walk into view behind us. The surprise and doubt on her face told me she could see the shadow of his spirit looming over us all. "It seems I may have misjudged you, Rose," she said. "I never would have guessed that the pretty cheerleader of a witch at that pathetic interfaith rally was capable of any real magic."

She was baiting me. Okay, fine. The longer we stood here squabbling, the more time the police had to show up and save our bacon.

"I like being under-estimated," I said. "I hope you keep it up." I looked at the men in black robes and then back at the scarlet-clad woman. "So, you are Templum Chaldeos. Doesn't that mean 'Temple of Babylon'?"

The woman turned her back on us and motioned for her overgrown altar boys to move into place near the children. As they slid across the circle, knife blades glinting in the candle flame, I realized that she trusted her circle to keep us at a distance.

"We can chit-chat after the show, precious," she said. "I'm sure we'll have so much to talk about." The kids whimpered as she turned her attention back on them. She held a halting finger up at us without turning to look in our direction. "I have work to do, sweethearts. Push me, and I'll skip ahead to the finale." The robed men put their daggers to the children's throats while she turned

184

back to the little girl, her black candle nearly overflowing with melted wax.

She was putting a lot of faith in her circle. Yes, it was supposed to be a boundary, but we'd already seen through it. What was to stop us from walking through, as well?

Lilly must have come to the same conclusion, because I saw her reach a hand toward the energetic perimeter at the same time as me. I felt a jolt and jerked my hand back. The crackle and pop reminded me of a giant bug zapper. I guess we were the mosquitoes.

Lilly smiled a wide, wicked smile. "Electricity," she laughed. I felt a flutter in my stomach. If we couldn't get through this electric fence, then neither could the police. Not in time, at any rate.

"I guess she didn't anticipate a weather witch knocking at her door," Lilly chuckled. She held her left hand toward the wall of sizzling energy and pointed her right hand toward the floor. "I love the lightning," she crowed as a visible charge coursed through her body and grounded into the floor below us. She slumped to her knees as the last trickle of energy left her fingertips.

Evaline and I charged toward the men, who were momentarily stunned. They might have been the ones wielding knives, but they were also weaker than their leader. They would be easier to intimidate. Evaline growled and lunged at the one near the boy. They went to the floor together somewhere behind me.

I faced my own robed goon and realized I was about to have my first knife fight. *Sweet, holy, fucking God! What am I doing? What do I do?* My mind reeled for a moment, and I saw the faces of the three victims claimed by these people. As I looked at the knife, now pointing at me and not the little girl, it occurred to me that the blade had almost certainly tasted the blood of this child's mother.

I could hear the mother's voice, rising like a whisper from the microscopic bits of blood that lingered on the knife. Like a ghostly chorus, it was joined by that of Lilly's turned-out roommate and the homeless man who had been slain on the east side of town.

I could hear the voices as they called for the blood of their killers. The look on the man's face told me he heard them, too.

Without preamble, he dropped the knife and ran. I had the momentary instinct to give chase. The girl at my side yelped, and I turned just in time to see the woman in red swing a knife downward at me from high above her head. I ducked the blade, and she lost her balance, stumbling into the spot where I had been standing. Unfortunately, that put her closer to the child.

She raised her knife again, and I felt Robin like an oncoming storm at my back. The woman in red froze under his gaze. "You've failed," he shouted. "Your master will not rise. You will not shed the blood of these innocents." Each sentence was a command, and with each command, he roared her another step back until she was standing at the center of the circle, the epicenter of the demon's sigil. Her curving dagger hung limply from her hand as she looked around the room.

Pearl had untied the boy, and they both now stood behind a renewed Lilly. Evaline had pinned her man to the ground, snarling and snapping at his throat each time he tried to move. The other man had vanished, his knife now in my hands to free the girl. Robin stood behind the woman, and she looked tiny and frail in his shadow.

The sound of police sirens reached us, thin and muffled by the concrete walls.

"I haven't failed," the woman mumbled. "I can't fail." She grasped her knife with both hands and pointed it at her own torso. "Take my blood as your final and greatest tribute, Dark King," she shouted and plunged the knife upward into the hollow place below her sternum.

Robin caught her as she fell and carried her outside the circle before a drop of her blood found the sigil beneath her. "Not that it would have mattered," he said to her as he laid her on the concrete. Her eyes fluttered. "Your blood is too sullied to satisfy the last component of this working. Your death is justice, not sacrifice." She closed her eyes just as Detective Jackson entered the room.

"Nobody move," he barked.

Chapter 28

It's a cliché to say that what happened next was a blur. Let's face it, though, all that happened in the next several hours and days was paperwork and questioning and getting everybody's stories on record. Very little of real interest happened, aside from discovering that Robin does indeed have DNA and fingerprints just like a real boy, neither of which were on file in any computer system on the planet. Nor did he have a driver's license or a National Insurance number, which is evidently the British equivalent of a Social Security number.

Actually, the lack of identification was no surprise to me, but it shocked the hell out of Detective Jackson. We spent the next several weeks talking with and being tested by a veritable host of federal agencies. The upshot of our long conference with a nest of bureaucrats is that Robin got his shots and tags, and the coven made some contacts in the FBI and Homeland Security, both of whom seem more eager to learn about witchcraft than they did a year ago.

Nobody in my coven was charged with any crime, and the whack-job, psycho-priestess and her remaining goon are awaiting trial. As I understand it, the goon has lost whatever mind he had before getting involved with *Templum Inferni*, which is what they actually called themselves. *Templum Chaldeos*, it seems, was a name they created for us when they wrote the manifesto trying to get us arrested in their stead. The manifesto was more or less true in terms of philosophy and methods, the names having been changed to protect the guilty.

Chapter 29

The brass bell above the door jingled as I sailed in, my messenger bag bulging with treats. Evaline finished ringing up a customer, and I plopped onto the squashy sofa between Lilly and Pearl.

"So, what's the big news?" Pearl asked.

"Not yet," I said. "Wait for Evie." I looked around. "Is Robin here yet? I don't see him."

Lilly shook her head. "He should be here soon. He said a friend was giving him a ride."

Robin still lived with Lilly and me, but his social circle had expanded significantly. We hadn't met many of his friends, though.

"How have readings been today?" I asked Lilly.

She nodded so vigorously that the seat bounced under us both. "So amazing," she said. "I can't believe how much I've learned since Evaline brought me into the shop."

"And the money?" Pearl asked.

"It's fine," Lilly grinned. She wasn't one to kiss and tell. "The shop as a whole has been doing fantastic since Evie took it over. She's got a good head for this."

"What about you, Rose?" Pearl asked. "Are the po-po paying you well for telling them all the witchy secrets?"

I shrugged. There was a joking tone to her voice, and she was only giving a playful voice to the insecurities I had about my new role. I tried not to sound as defensive as I felt when I said, "I'm not telling them all the witchy secrets. I'm not really telling them anything that is meant to be secret. The Mysteries can't be communicated, after all. I'm just consulting with them on cases involving magic-users."

Damn. I sucked at not sounding defensive.

"Calm your tits," Pearl said, rolling her eyes. "You know I'm only kidding. Don't be so sensitive."

I flopped my head on her shoulder. "I'm sensitive," I pouted. She patted the top of my head. "How's Miss Bea?" I asked.

"Rotten," Pearl sighed and rolled her eyes. "She's fine. Dramatic and seven and fine."

We all sat in silence for a moment before Lilly asked, "Has anybody heard from Grace lately?"

Pearl and I both shook our heads. Grace had officially ended our relationship, unofficially withdrawn from the coven, and announced her permanent relocation to her parents' home on the border of Kentucky. "I haven't been healthy up there for a while," she had texted. "I love you all, and this is my own issue, but I can't do it anymore. I hope someday you will forgive me."

There was no room to argue. No reason to argue, either. We missed Grace, but she really hadn't been stable or happy with me, with us, for a long time. If she could find joy and foundation with her family, she should try.

Lilly, Pearl, and I heaved a collective sigh.

Evaline glided over to us and perched on one of the chairs. "As soon as Robin gets here, I'm locking the door and pouring a glass of wine."

The brass bell jingled.

"Speak of the devil," I said, perking up after my momentary lull, "and he doth appear."

Robin looked so magnificent in his dove grey suit, that I almost didn't see the man following him to our nook. Almost.

"Ladies," Robin swept a short bow to the three of us on the couch while Evie locked the door and pulled the shade. "I'd like to introduce you to Jack," he said. The tall, broad-shouldered, eyepatch-wearing friend shook each of our hands in turn. "Jack is *family*," Robin said, using the traditional introduction. "And a very old line of the family it is. He's in real estate, isn't that right?"

Jack nodded. He looked a little more like a bouncer than a broker. Those shoulders were very broad. "Sorry to crash your gathering," he said. He looked sheepish.

"I insisted he come," Robin interjected. "It was time you met."

I felt my head cock to one side like a confused terrier, but before I had time to pry, Robin said, "Rose, tell us your news."

I clutched my bag close to my chest for a second before pulling the items out one by one and displaying them on the glass coffee table. A bottle of champagne. A box of chocolates.

"Ooh," Pearl giggled. "Rose is proposing to us!"

I shook my head and pulled a thick stack of paper out. The manuscript was neatly bound in string with the title page gleaming.

Thrice the Circle

A Novel

By Rose Wheeler

Lilly clapped and Evaline squealed. "Oh, my goat! You finished your book. That's incredible."

"I didn't just finish it," I said, pulling one more goody from my bag. "I've been offered a publishing contract for it."